Sparkman in the Sky
& Other Stories

Sparkman in the Sky & Other Stories

Brian Griffin

Winner of the 1996
Mary McCarthy Prize in Short Fiction
Selected by Barry Hannah

Sarabande Books
LOUISVILLE, KENTUCKY

Managing Editor
Sarabande Books, Inc.
2234 Dundee Road, Suite 200
Louisville, KY 40205

LIBRARY OF CONGRESS CATALOGING-IN-PUBLICATION DATA

Griffin, Brian, 1957–
    Sparkman in the sky and other stories / by Brian Griffin. — 1st ed.
        p.   cm.
    ISBN 1-889330-05-1 (acid-free paper). — ISBN 1-889330-06-X (pbk. :
acid-free paper).
    1. Southern States—Social life and customs—Fiction. I. Title.
PS3557.R48865S67   1997
813' .54—dc21   96-39817
                                                                              CIP

Cover painting: *My Vietnam* by Jack Chevalier,
used with the permission of the artist.

Cover and text design by Charles Casey Martin.

Manufactured in the United States of America.
This book is printed on acid-free paper.

Sarabande Books is a nonprofit literary organization.

To Amy

Acknowledgments

New Delta Review: "Big Ash"

Shenandoah: "Sparkman in the Sky," "A Few Casualties"

Snake Nation Review: "Home for the Weekend"

Special thanks to John Casey, George Garrett, Rita Dove, Fred Viebahn, Eleanor Ross Taylor, Larry Mapp, Dabney Stuart, Pat Strachan, and Sarah Gorham for guidance and wisdom second only to the far different wisdom of my children, Ezra and Miriam. And to Amy, Jackie, Cliff, and Wayne—thanks for believing.

■

In memory of Peter Taylor

Contents

Foreword
The Splendid Mr. Griffin

The Griffin stories are remarkable. Without the hectoring and false tones you might find in yet another chronicle of cozy or lunatic Dixiana, Griffin offers a natural persuasion about these citizens in Tennessee. Mostly the voice comes to him as easily as a walk through the park, it seems, and I find this an imperative in writers of the first order. I hold that in all the best writing there is a natural pace, an unwilled but inevitable current. We do not want the manufactured feeling, the forced plastic, the strains of bogus rhetoric. But we want idealized conversation, as many have said. No writer gets it all the time, certainly not yours truly in his own stories.

But Griffin gets it often enough. My wife, not especially literary but smart in better ways, was sitting among a lot of manuscripts on the rug in her study, thousands of pages in stacks around her, when she lifted up some sheets from Brian Griffin. "Say, this one can write," she cheered. I'd already made my choice but one always fears his own prejudice. I can't bear consciously "smart" fiction, for instance, in the way that it is hard for me not to detest (unfairly) the child of a bragging parent. How about letting *me* find out if the kid's smart, all right? My wife is a Californian and wants "just a good story" in the books she reads. So I was pleased to be abetted by her in my choice for the Sarabande contest. Mr. Griffin should know that he's been thoroughly vetted by various and improbable judges, like Miss America.

I think the stories are good because Griffin has listened to them before he began writing them. Stories should be deeply felt and should speak *to* the writer, so that his translation to us is almost helpless. In that way all superior narrative fiction is "automatic," and you often hear of the best being written at great speed. I sense the author has lived the life and is barely staying up with the events, like a gasping court reporter. And this is good.

Good too is the anarchy in the stories. It is fine that the chronicler is not fully aware of all he has on his hand, and that he wanders a little. Not a lot, not in scatterbrained reeling, not back-scratching filibuster, not just writing *writing,* as Norman Mailer once called it, but in *some* uncertainty as to where this life is leading. Otherwise you get what America has too much of now: nicely crafted fiction, book after book. There is a sameness to books nowadays that is an awful curiosity in the land of freedom. Huge and discouraging conformity. Sometimes I feel fiction might as well be all from the old Soviet Union. With absolute freedom of ideas, American writers keep stamping out redundant blocks of, well, social realism worse than good newspapers. The authorship is interchangeable, as in a factory of the infinite. Thank God Griffin and a few others are different and distinct, not just for novelty but for the distinction in human life and blood. He knows, as all honest writers do, that the anarchy of the planet is likely to rush in and bust up your little story at any given time. That you are barely holding onto it. Vide "Sparkman." Yes, the story might have come from the *precincts* of Flannery O'Connor—the senile preacher, the crippled boy, his slanderous dreams. But Griffin creates his own distinct life from Southern stock. Our grand gestures against hidebound geezers always come too late. The story might as well be about writing. Our enemies are always dead and safe by the time we've become wise enough to outrage them. A powerful story.

It seems that every choice for the larger world brings disaster among Griffin's people. I've often held that the Civil War was caused by boredom as much as anything. Drive through the small burgs of the South and you will support me. But adventure is perilous. In fact, ruinous. The Army always beckons to the men and is the main exotic exit from local tedium or teenage bafflement. Uncle Sam wants you, and in almost every case he wants all of you. Maimed and crazed or just punked-out, returning veterans are never whole. Griffin has it right about the little burgs, too. Outside the shuffling quotidian of their lives, the people often have only the continuity of wars for their history. Southerners make the best warriors, I have decided after vast reading in military history. They like to fight. This may be awful. But you get the idea that several thousand of them have jumped on boats all rowdy to blow hell out of the other side and were apprised of who the enemy was only about mid-journey. The Zulus, the Celts, the Scots, Goths, and Huns—us. Nevertheless, life in the service is real and singular to them. Back home there are just a few chores, a few girls, maybe a little sport.

The women in these tales have considerable power. I remember that wonderful telephone ringing on the dock with the boy in the boat, on his way to the Army, another lost connection to love. As with Dixie Pepper, a woman of the sticks with great wicked anarchy in her. She seems to have remained at home *only* to wreck normal life,

like an angry big fish in a little pond. Then there are the dangerous
girls with Webb who confront the quivering square narrating
"Training to Be an Astronaut." Enormous fun, even as I now recall:
all women herein are dangerous and dodgy. There is not a single
comfortable sexual act in the book.

Nor are sports mere dalliances. Baseball is a killer in a great story
of floundering church youth and their floundering mentors. A
church steeple is sawed off. People get voracious and weird, but not
quaint, thank God.

Griffin has laid out a rich and deep patch of Griffin territory,
somewhere around Chattanooga, between the city and the country,
that will be remembered. Sometimes when forced to answer that
dreadful question about why the South produces such fine writers,
after a mild vomiting spell, I say, "Well, maybe because the choices
are so few: religion, sports, wars, girls, weather." The very paucity
that should wreck every sensitive soul, according to sensitive soci-
ologers, is exactly what they need. They have time to concentrate,
and their daydreams walk in and take over.

Most of all, Griffin's stories are great deep fun.

Barry Hannah
Oxford, Mississippi
August, 1996

Sparkman in the Sky
& Other Stories

Sparkman in the Sky

L et no man claim to know the mind of God, how He makes things collide or diverge, or what is His design—this is the kind of statement Sparkman scribbles on the pages of the Reverend Grandfather's morning paper. This is Sparkman's war. "Let no man fly higher than his purpose, which may be lower than mud," he wrote in a Nancy comic strip, inside Sluggo's thought balloon. "The man who has no grave is covered by the sky."

Each morning before sunrise, even before the delivery boy flings the *Chattanooga Times* against the side of the trailer, Sparkman is lying awake in bed, waiting naked in the moonglow. A ceiling fan slices above him, pushing heat against his skin. His fingers run along his belly and thighs, up along the pocked scars of surgery that cross his white chest like iced trails. Somehow he always knows when the delivery boy turns the curve near the catfish pond and begins to pedal up the driveway. Maybe the sound of the crickets gives it away, a slight drag in their rhythm. Maybe it's something vaguely electric that tickles across the air into the trailer itself, coming to rest in Sparkman's skull. Maybe it's magic. But always he knows. If he chooses, he can snap his finger in the split second before the newspaper thumps against the door.

So each morning when he senses the approach of the delivery boy, Sparkman limps down the tiny hallway, his right leg sweeping across the linoleum, balling up puffs of dust. The Reverend Grandfather's snores tumble along the walls, grumpy little spirits oozing through the stale air, little pious growls. The walls of the hallway are lined with black-and-white pictures of tents, the revival tents the Reverend used back in his younger days. There were three different tents over a period of thirty-one years but they all look the same, and for years Sparkman has had an urge to add paint to those pictures, to make them glow a bright vivid orange the way he remembers them. He remembers the sawdust, the musk of it in the air, the grit of it on his skin. The sawdust sometimes stuck in his hair or filled his mouth when he fell on his face. Lots of times he would fall without warning. One minute he'd be at the piano playing "I'll Fly Away" or "The Old Rugged Cross," or maybe he'd be sitting stiff in the amen corner, Bible in hand, watching the Reverend Grandfather's squeezing red face spew out the word of God for all to bathe in; and suddenly he would find himself on his back in the sawdust with a spoon in his mouth and tense arch-browed old ladies waving funeral-home fans in his face, cardboard fans shaped like turkeys or peacocks, or maybe with faces of famous dead men printed on them, and those funeral fans seemed to push him to the earth, pinning him down, as if to keep him from drifting too high above the sawdust and the aluminum chairs and the round-eyed quivering ladies. And beyond those ladies and their pulsing fans, high above them in a milky haze of dust and ill-light, stretched the orange underside of the tent, a musty canvas sky. Beyond that sky were stars or moon or sun or blue air, the very heavens—while all that orbited for Sparkman, he

4

thought, were those blabbering faces adrift in their orange sky, and perhaps a flash of the Reverend: eyes closed, arms spread high toward the orange canvas of heaven, his lips churning out packets of magic for all under the big top to fondle. He was a healer all right, and Sparkman was his most valuable asset. All that's left of those tents now, years after the Reverend Grandfather's retirement, is a muddy fragment of tarp over the woodpile behind the trailer—and, of course, the pictures in the hallway, along which Sparkman creeps each morning. "The benevolence of God? The fruits of His labor?" Sparkman once scribbled in the Society section. "Luck is everything."

Sparkman always knows what he will write in the Reverend Grandfather's newspaper. It just takes a second. The door swings out and he snatches the paper from beside the potted banana tree on the porch. He stands naked in the open door, bone-thin and white in the first glow of dawn, his lame right leg twisted beneath him. In the thin light he can see the stone chimney of the home place rising from the depression where the house once stood, a few feet in front of where the trailer is now. The house burned when Sparkman was ten years old, while he and the Reverend Grandfather were in Pulaski preaching to coal miners under the orange tent, making them sweat.

Sparkman slides the rubber band down the rolled newspaper. It makes a plinking noise, the sound of a slackened harp string. He folds out the paper, opens to a random page, and writes his message quickly with his left hand. He rolls the paper again, strums the rubber band to its place, returns to bed. It's become easy, second nature; the way one might toss out a tired old cat.

Sparkman has started a revolution. The biggest step, of course, was his decision to attend college, the new community college on Buckton Pike. It's walking distance for Sparkman, along a narrow country road.

It was built on land once owned by Sparkman's family, part of a huge farm settled and cleared and built by the Reverend Grandfather's father. Most of the land has long since been frittered away, though. All they have left is a tiny lot surrounded by someone else's cows.

Sparkman studies music, philosophy, but mostly accounting; has his eye on hang-gliding. Big Al keeps turning him down for hang gliding, though, citing his medical history, claiming his body won't fit the harness, claiming he doesn't weigh enough, whatever he can think of. "I'm sorry," says Big Al. He reaches down and slaps Sparkman's shoulder, popping his gum. His teeth glow like piano keys. "Sorry, big guy. Really."

Big Al is never really sorry, though; Sparkman knows that. Big Al, he thinks, is a health Nazi, a Specimen, blond-haired, blue-eyed, full of raging Wheaties and muscled sperm. The kind of guy who could have modeled for Hitler's sculptors if Hitler hadn't lost the war. Big Al runs the bike shop, eats lots of fiber, gives weekend hang gliding lessons through the college. He teaches the basics in a pasture near Sparkman's trailer and then has everybody jump from Rebel's Roost on Lookout Mountain, site of the Battle Above the Clouds. If General Bragg had had hang gliders, says Big Al, the Rebels never would've lost Missionary Ridge.

Sparkman's been bent like a question mark since birth. He blacks out frequently, takes lots of medicine, walks with a limp. He keeps showing up at the hang gliding lessons, though, waiting for some magic chance, hoping Big Al might change his mind. Sparkman was elated the first time he saw hang gliders in the pasture. They flew with a grace he could feel, like a chill running along his spine. He limped across the yard to the pasture, flapping his arms gently in the warm July air, trying to imagine what it would be like to fly. When he got closer, though, he was surprised. They didn't have wheels.

6

He'd seen pictures of gliders with wheels, like flying chariots, but these were more like butterflies.

■

Sometimes Big Al lets Sparkman take the glider parts from their long nylon bags, helping him assemble the gliders on the crest of the grassy hill. From there Sparkman can see cattle on the rolling hills below, the curving road as it ducks into the thin stand of hickory, the community college on the other side of the trees, and of course the trailer, which looks small next to the stone chimney of the home place; he can see the dark green of Walden's Ridge and, on a clear day, even Lookout Mountain to the south, blue in the distance. Big Al winks as Sparkman hands him the thin aluminum poles, the nylon sails, the harness strapping. "It's a beauty," Big Al says. "A real beaut."

After the assembly, Sparkman leans against a fencepost at the bottom of the hill as the bright orange gliders lift their pilots into the air, gently, like dandelion seed. Sometimes the wind takes them high, frames them against the clouds. Sparkman always watches alone, from a distance. He clutches his philosophy textbook to his chest, curling around it as the gliders drift across the pasture. And Big Al always comes to Sparkman afterward. "How's it, Sparky?" he would say. "How's studies? How's life treating you?"

Sparkman just stares at his text.

Big Al reaches down, plucks a blade of grass, puts it in the corner of his mouth. "Well then," he says. "How's the Old Man?"

"Older," Sparkman says. He adjusts his glasses and looks up at Big Al, at his twinkly blue eyes.

Big Al laughs. "Easier to fool?"

Sparkman shrugs.

Sometimes Sparkman helps load the nylon glider bags into the van and rides to the college with Big Al. Big Al smiles, talks about vegetables and jogging. He offers Sparkman apples or sun-dried apricots. Sparkman refuses, sullen as always, looking out the window. They store the bagged gliders on shelves beneath the gymnasium bleachers, and Sparkman returns to his books.

Sparkman spends hours with his books. That in itself is revolutionary. These days the Reverend Grandfather seems to have forgotten the college, the blasphemy of it; the way it teaches alien values; the way it has usurped some of the old family land. With time he has grown distant, estranged, as if he has merged with the trailer, oozed across it one too many times and blended into the wall like an old photograph. He hardly seems to care anymore that people are going to hell all around him—or to heaven without his blessing. He's signed over the bank accounts to Sparkman, and he's relinquished his control over Sparkman's Social Security checks. He no longer goes to church. He no longer burns Sparkman's books. He no longer preaches to Sparkman about the evils of secular humanism. All these things are revolutions in Sparkman's world. Dismantlings. Unthinkables. In fact, the Reverend Grandfather seems totally uninterested in Sparkman these days. Almost as if he doesn't know him anymore.

So after thirty-one years of mute, unquestioning awe—awe of God, awe of Reverend Grandfather, awe of the lilting, levitating pulpit of Bucktooth Haven Baptist Church—Sparkman has begun asking questions. He sits for hours with his philosophy textbook and wonders about things. Was it all illusion, shadows of the mind? Is there nothing but matter, mind, self? Does the buck stop here, in this squiggly body and churning skull? The questions come thick and fast as he reads Plato and Sartre; just asking such questions is gratifying for Sparkman in a deep physical way, like his first massage from a professional masseuse (a massage which came, incidentally, after reading Camus) and for a while it seems he's found old beams of light that had been hidden and scattered and diminished in a long eclipse; a cluster of desiccated truths, like old fruit that was kept from him, left to parch and wrinkle and shrink. What might have happened, he asks, had he found them succulent and whole, in some earlier time? What might have happened had he known?

So, almost without realizing it, Sparkman has set for himself what once had seemed an unthinkable task: the deconstruction, the demystification, the reeducation of the Reverend Grandfather. The most powerful man in Sparkman's world. The man with The Plan, the man they call Eli. The man whose mouth makes the shapes, whose arms make the moves, as if God is a ventriloquist. "Sod for the harrow, feed for the sparrow, no special passage," Sparkman writes in a Sunday edition, above a photo of Charlton Heston. "The road to heaven is equally short from all places." He circles it, makes it into a thought balloon emerging from the actor's forehead. A kind of revenge.

At breakfast the Reverend Grandfather sits at the kitchen table with his newspaper and Bible. "Elijah!" the Reverend Grandfather says. A matter-of-fact statement, not directed at anyone in particular. His voice is harsh, like steam from a valve.

Sparkman stands beside him with the syringe. He pokes it under the powdery skin. The Reverend is wide-eyed, oblivious. He scrunches up his nose and puffs air through his nostrils.

The Sunday paper is open on the table before the Reverend Grandfather. A full bottle of insulin sits on the table beside the salt and pepper. The Reverend clutches his damp, warm Bible under the pit of his right arm, the injection arm. Tiny black eyes look up at Sparkman.

"Elijah!" says the Reverend Grandfather. His horn-rimmed glasses slide down his nose, resting even with his cheeks.

"Would you like some strawberry jam?" Sparkman says.

The Reverend's eyebrows arch, hairy tepees form on his forehead.

"More sugar in your coffee, Reverend Grandfather?"

The Reverend Grandfather's face narrows, his forehead stretches upward. He is thin. "Skin and bones," the church ladies say when they bring plate lunches in the afternoons. Mrs. Thrasher always remembers to wind the wooden clock that hangs above the kitchen table.

Sparkman smiles at the Reverend Grandfather. The Reverend rubs his gums together, licks his lips. The ticking of the clock makes his temples pulse. His skin is a sail; dry fabric stretched across segments of bone.

"Elijah!"

"A very lucky man," says Sparkman.

Sparkman rises from the table and walks to the television. He puts a tape in the VCR, turns on the set, rolls it up to the table. He lifts the set, places it on the table in front of the Reverend, and turns off the volume. The Reverend spits, a long trail of spittle dangling above his coffee cup. He lifts his head, his mouth hangs open. His eyes fix on the set. It's a movie about airplanes: fuzzy black-and-white films of planes that never got off the ground. Some have multilayered wings that flap and break themselves to pieces like caged birds. Some are thin frameworks of wood and canvas that fall from cliffs like stone. A goggled man in a dark suit and tie runs along a field, wings strapped to his arms. The wings flap, the man runs, the man jumps from a cliff to the ocean.

The Reverend Grandfather floats above his coffee cup.

"Can I get you a glazed doughnut, Reverend Grandfather?"

The Reverend's pale skin glows in the light of the television. "Luck?" he says. His tongue seems to stick to his lips.

"How about a nice slice of cheesecake?"

10

The Reverend's head swivels around toward Sparkman. "Elijah," he says. "ELI-JAH!"

As the tape rewinds, Sparkman decides to leave. Often Sparkman sits with his books on the wooden bleachers in the college gymnasium. Sometimes Big Al shows up, does a few push-ups, runs a few laps. Other times groups of girls would be there, playing volleyball. Sparkman likes the bounce and sweat and grace of the girls' bodies, the way they fly into the air to swat the ball, the way their arms swing wide to embrace the air, the way their voices echo across the gym floor like the cries of seabirds. Sparkman likes to imagine how they might feel if he touched them. He imagines them soft, hot, and light to the touch, able to float high into the sky if he simply pushed. A tiny push would do it.

The gym is full of girls when Sparkman arrives. Even a few boyfriends are standing around. Sparkman sits on the bleachers and begins to read, but soon he's staring at the girls. He can't help it. After a while the boyfriends stare at Sparkman. Finally one of them walks toward him, his boots sharp and crisp on the wooden gym floor. Sparkman hears the boyfriends snicker. He leaves his books and walks beneath the bleachers, and he can hear the boots. He can hear the sounds of the girls at volleyball, and he can hear the boots much closer now. Sparkman squats beside the shelves where the gliders are stored and leans back on his heels as the boots get very close. Sparkman closes his eyes, and the sound of the boots stops. Sparkman waits, his hands clenched across his knees. His head hurts from the reading, his leg aches, he's covered in sweat. After a minute Sparkman hears the boots walk away, and he leans against the smooth nylon of a glider bag, cool against his arm like a gentle lick across the skin.

He rubs his fingers along the bag, his face pressed against the orange fabric. Then he puts his arms around the glider and slides it to the very edge of its shelf. He looks quickly over his shoulder, then bends his knees. He can feel the beat of his heart even in his wrists as he lifts the orange glider bag and balances it on his right shoulder. He stands for a second, steadying himself. Aluminum rods bulge beneath the fabric like hollow bones, hard against his skin. Sparkman turns slightly and looks behind him; then slowly, carefully, he walks toward the gym floor. The boyfriends talk among themselves; the girls bounce around the net. Giggles are everywhere, but nobody notices him. Bold, audacious, in broad daylight, Sparkman walks across the gym floor toward the door. He simply walks out of the gymnasium, carrying the glider out into the heat. He crosses a parking lot and enters woods, limping along, the long glider balanced on his shoulder. He leans under its weight, his right arm flexed around it.

The shade is a gentle sigh. He smiles, giddy at the ease of it, the surprise of it. He finds a faint footpath that runs beside a dry streambed. After a minute, he sets the glider down and rests on a stone. He's breathing hard, his chest hurts. He looks at the glider, runs his hands across the smooth nylon bag, and looks toward the sky. Chunks of sunlight tumble through the branches, and Sparkman can almost feel the licks of gentle air that would loft him up, etching him into the sky above the wide green pasture. He would wear a cloak, flapping behind him in rippling waves. Below him would be the trailer, and he would circle it, lifting, spiraling upward. Then he would dive swiftly toward the old chimney, arcing up just before colliding with stone. At that instant he would see the birds' nests on the chimneytop, the speckles and cracks of the eggs, the tiny bits of fluff that line the nests. And below him would be the Reverend Grandfather, standing outside the trailer door in the shadow of the stone chimney, his neck bent back, his long face shining red, his eyes blinking white and round into the sky, a beacon. Sparkman would loop around the trailer once and then descend toward the Reverend's face. Perhaps he would grab him by the shoulders with his feet, plucking him from the earth like a plant, pulling up whatever root might be there and letting it dangle. Or perhaps he would drop his cloak, letting it flutter through the air, letting it drape the shining face. Then the air would lift him up again. Very high up. Above the clouds, perhaps. Sparkman grins. He stands, lifts the glider, and begins to walk. The weight of the glider rubs hot against his shoulder.

The woods grow thicker as he walks. Thick second growth. The long bag bumps against tree trunks, snags on branches. Sweat drenches his body in the still air. He hears rustlings and snappings in the trees and weeds, as though he is being followed. Sweat drips from his forehead, sprinkling the dry dirt of the trail. A rusty strand of barbed wire trips him, the trail fades away. He walks along the dry stones of the creekbed. Finally he emerges from the trees, dragging the bright orange glider along the road behind him. The weeds along the roadside rustle with insects.

But no one sees him, or if they see him they think nothing of it. When Sparkman arrives home he leans the glider against the chimney in front of the trailer and stands for a second, waiting. Nothing happens, so Sparkman enters and finds the Reverend Grandfather sitting at the kitchen table, staring at a blank television screen. Sparkman takes the Reverend Grandfather by the arm. The Reverend quivers as he stands. Both cold dry hands grasp hard to Sparkman's arm. The Reverend says nothing. His eyeglasses are covered in dust. Sparkman leads him out into the sunlight, and the Reverend blinks his eyes.

Sparkman leads him to the sunken grassy spot in front of the old chimney. He points to the sky. "Look up," Sparkman says. The Reverend Grandfather looks into the cloudless sky. His mouth falls open for a second, but Sparkman pushes on the jaw, and it stays shut.

13

Sparkman lifts the glider to his shoulder and carries it across the pasture toward the crest of the hill. The grass is thick, in big clumps, and Sparkman walks very slowly in the heat. The hill slopes gently for a long way before rising sharply to the summit.

About halfway up the steep part, Sparkman drops the glider to the grass and bends at his waist with his hands on his knees. Sweat drips silently from the tip of his nose into the dry grass. His sweat knocks a small grasshopper from its perch, and the grasshopper squirms in the lower grass before flying away with a buzzing sound. Sparkman hears thunder somewhere across the mountains, but no clouds are in sight. A slight breeze begins to stir. Sparkman rubs his hand along the calf of his right leg and drops to his knees in the grass. He's gone as far as he can go. He assembles the glider where he is, on a steep slope about twenty-five yards below the crest of the hill.

Thirty minutes later, Sparkman squats beneath the glider, his skin glowing orange in the filtered light. Puffs of wind make the glider feel alive, like some rebellious piece of skin tugging him up from the earth. His hands, slick with sweat, clutch hard to the control bar. He can't fit himself into the harness, so he figures he'll just have to hang on, dangling from the control bar by his arms. He knows he won't be able to steer very well, hanging there that way. If he goes through with this, he thinks, he'll just have to hold hard to the bar and hope. He'll just have to hope the breeze lifts him gently, not too high, and sends him in the right direction.

He can see the trailer below. Two dark birds fly from the ruined chimney, circle the trailer, then disappear back into the chimney, over and over again. The Reverend Grandfather stands where Sparkman left him, looking into the sky. There's a wide space between them, but Sparkman can see him fairly well: the violent crook of his neck, the upturned paleness of his face, the smallness of his body in the sunken

14

patch of grass beside the chimney. Sparkman waves his arm in a wide loop, trying to catch his grandfather's attention, but the Reverend doesn't see him. It's as if he doesn't even see the hill, as if he is looking higher, much higher than Sparkman. But Sparkman continues to squat beneath the glider, waving, his left hand moving in wide arcs, his right hand grasping the control bar. Finally he begins to yell into the shifting air. The glider is a piece of his skin, teasing him, tugging at him with each breath of air. The breeze comes, then dies down, then comes again, and Sparkman feels each gust deep inside, as if the glider were attached by strings to something deep in his belly. And suddenly Sparkman realizes how easy it would be—how he could just stand up and lean into one of the gusts, and that would be it. He could just stand up and push forward and leave the earth, going up, across the open air. With a single step forward, he could fly.

Sparkman begins to tremble and his lips spread out in a smile, and his hands grip the control bar. The wind blows hard now, and he feels his legs tighten and his heart jump, and his smile goes away. Again Sparkman yells but the Reverend Grandfather stares into the air, hearing nothing, seeing nothing, and the wind keeps blowing.

There seems to be too much space. The birds fly in circles around the trailer, wide loops outside the Reverend's field of vision, around and around the trailer. Sparkman feels the gusting wind, harder, and the teasing again, almost violent now, and he sees the long wide slope covered with grass and the trailer far below. The Reverend Grandfather stands small beside the chimney, and there is that wide, wide space. There is that little man, and there is everything he knows. And he knows it's just too far away, much too far.

So Sparkman stands and steps into the wind.

Big Ash

Lightning killed it. It had been as good as dead for two seasons but nobody would admit it. Finally they decided it might tip over and smash some headstones, so on the morning of Karlen's funeral they took it out. They cut it low to the ground, and later they covered the stump with dirt left over from Karlen's grave; then after a while some crab grass came and covered the dirt.

You'd think losing something that big, right at the center of things, would make the whole place seem new. But no, it just made a big empty spot in the sky, that's all, so that only the sky itself seemed new. Everything below the sky just seemed a little bit shoddier and more raggedy and a little bit deader to look at—the way it always was, only worse. I guess I should've known better, to even think that way. Karlen would've slapped my shoulder and winked his sparkle-eye and said, "Now Newt, you know better than thinking that shit. What's the use of thinking that shit?" and his eyes would beam out at me and his lips would grin tight across his teeth or across his bare-hole gums, maybe, if those teeth were already gone the way they finally did go, and he'd say, "Fine. Think fine. Everything's fine."

■

From Karlen's place, you could see the cemetery. Early in the morning the day of his funeral I stood at the chain-link fence at the edge of Karlen's land, watching them dismantle that big ash piece by piece with a crane. There were these two monkey kinds of guys with chain saws hopping from limb to limb, tying them off and cutting in close to the trunk, and then the crane swung the big limbs out from the main trunk, stacking them on a flatbed truck. That's what they were doing instead of digging Karlen's hole. They were taking that big ash apart like they had all the time in the world, like it was a big Tinkertoy, like it was first things first. Those chain saws were screams, so I reached behind my ear and flicked the switch, turning off the sound. Now they were just a gnarling belly, and still I could feel them ripping across the morning air, making a tingle on my skin.

Karlen's Aunt Maggie was behind me planting tomatoes, like Karlen wasn't even dead, like it was any other day and it wasn't even going to happen. Karlen's been like a child to her, and here he is about to get buried that very day and she plants tomatoes. I turned around and watched her and she ignored me. I was the best friend Karlen O'Malley ever had and she always ignored me, so I always just ignored her back. Karlen and me were like brothers, but Aunt Maggie was in her own little world, floating around Karlen's house like a motion picture shining on the walls.

I watched her plant those tomatoes for a while. She was small and dry now, shriveled up and rattly looking, and her hair was gray and hanging in thin floating strands. She had a tin bucket full of potion.

She would put a sprout in the dirt, then pour on some potion, over and over again, right down the row.

I could've taken off work but I didn't, I don't know why. A bunch of the other guys did. Instead I just left Maggie alone with her tomatoes, walked to the plant, and clocked in—like it was any other day. All day it was like Karlen was around somewhere puttering with the pipes instead of getting dropped six feet in a hole. Karlen was like that, able to spread himself around so all you had to do was say hello to him in the morning and he was there all day in the air around you, even though you couldn't see him. I'd said hello to him so many times over the years I didn't need to anymore. Even with him dead he was in the air, except maybe now there was a jagged edge to it I hadn't noticed before, an empty spot. All that morning I left the sound off, so when people said things to me I just looked back at them and went on with the mop or the broom or whatever, not making out much of what they said, and they'd either know or not know, and I didn't much care. It's really not so unusual for me to turn off the sound, I guess, I do it all the time. It's always for a reason.

Me and Karlen went to high school together and volunteered for the Army together and came home alive together and took this nuke-plant job together like we did everything else together, although Karlen never spent time at the V.A. Hospital the way I did. But he visited me a lot and he made sure they fixed me up right. It's Top Secret what happened to me in the Army, but everybody knows I can't hear very well and I'm always real shaky and sometimes big scabs come up on my skin. It was my duty, that's all. Karlen was big on that, and me too. When I got out of the V.A. Karlen made damn sure they hired me at that new nuclear plant the government was building, which is where Karlen ended up working after he left the Army. Of course, his Aunt Maggie didn't want Karlen near that nuclear plant from day one, claiming it would kill him, but Karlen just laughed and said, "Bullshit." And like I said, he even fixed things so they'd hire me too, even though it was just pushing a broom. But I didn't mind. Whatever it takes, I'll do it. I'm a team player, I play by the rules. Even ants have drones. Hell, ants *are* drones. Karlen, he was a damn good pipe man, the best one they had, and pipes is what keeps these things from melting down.

Karlen always was a wild-ass, and that's what got us in the Army and got us stuck out on a damn hunk of coral in the Pacific blowing things up—Karlen's being a wild-ass. Like, sometimes he would take poison ivy fresh out of the woods and rub it all over his skin and never even itch—he did it at basic training at Fort Bragg and he did it at home too, whenever he could get some fool to lay a bet on it. In the Army he volunteered us both for special trench duty just so he could see what it would look like from up close when one of those A-bombs blew, and he even snuck in a camera and made some pictures from way up close, but they came out mostly washed out and shaky—in two or three of them you could make out somebody's nose or arm or helmet but that's about it. Then he volunteered for something so secret even I didn't know, so I volunteered for some more special trench duty and that's when it happened, though I can't tell any more than that because it's Top Secret.

One time a bunch of us from the nuke plant went out to Darnell's Dive Den for some beer. I had the sound on. I always kept the sound on when we all went drinking with Karlen, even if somebody'd been giving me grief all day. Karlen, he got to bragging to the whole bar about how he was specially exempt from things that would put most folks under the table, and how poison ain't always poison and sickness ain't always sickness, how it's all attitude. Attitude and Maggie's potions, he'd say, Maggie's rabbit-tooth and spring-water potions, they'll ward off anything. He told how one time he got bit by a rat-tlesnake but it was no big deal, he bit it back, and it was like biting into a marshmallow that had sat out all night. That snake cried "Uncle" and Karlen said "Suck!" and it started sucking out that poi-son and Karlen was okay. Karlen was always bragging like that and everybody thought it was all right because it was a big joke the way he said it. Darnell though, he heard Karlen talking about rubbing himself with poison ivy and, being from Virginia and new in the bar business and not really one of us, Darnell bet Karlen he wouldn't do it. So Karlen grinned and said, "Hell, I'll do you one better." So he went outside and got some poison ivy and rubbed it on his arms. Then he went back in Darnell's kitchen and boiled a few leaves of it like it was turnip greens and put it on some cornbread and ate some of it with his beer. He won a hundred dollars from Darnell and bought beer for everybody and then put forty-eight dollars and sev-enty-six cents in the tip jar. I know for a fact Karlen spent all night throwing up, but he was at the plant the very next day, red-faced and grinning and slapping shoulders and saying, "Hi, nice day ain't it, nice day ain't it?" I had a hangover like hammers in my head, the kind that pounds on you, and he put his arm across my shoulders and looked straight at my eyes, grinning sly with his sparkle-eyes jump-ing out at me and that tobacco in his cheek, and he says, "It's the thinking about it, that's all." He grins and winks and says, "Poison is like politics, it ain't what it seems like. Take it in small enough doses and you get immune."

But something finally got him, years later. When it got really bad he wouldn't let the doctors treat him the way it should've been. He thought the first tumor was one of those scabs like both of us get, just floating on the surface, no big deal. But instead it sort of sawed through his arm into his bone and got inside him and spread around, and really that was the end, amputation or no amputation. After the amputation he ignored the doctors, ignored everybody. No chemo, no radiation treatments, he wouldn't allow it. I wonder if maybe Maggie made him that way, if she was behind it somehow. Sometimes it seemed like she thought everybody and everything was out to do Karlen in—cold beer, red meat, cholesterol, the nuclear plant, even the doctors who were trying their best to fix Karlen up. I saw the way her mouth froze up, the way her eyes poked through the air at those doctors. Her eyes could jab that way, making you dangle in front of her like a doll. One time when a little wire-rimmed doctor came in and told Karlen he should have radiation treatments, Maggie said, "Ain't that what got him sick in the first place?" So the doctor started to explain how the radiation would *kill* cancer cells and she said, "I know all that, but that *is* what got him. You know damn well it is." And the doctor, he says, "Well, in fact, it isn't. Nobody knows what caused it. It could've been anything," and Maggie just laughed at him. And I guess the real problem was that, by then, Karlen was feeling pretty good, because he laughed too. He had his color in his cheeks and he was ready for work, so he just laid there in that hospital bed and grinned at that little white-coat guy and said, "Now this radiation treatment—that would be like giving a drink of water to a drowning man, now wouldn't it, Doc?" And Karlen laughed a smiling kind of laugh and said, "You're all right, Doc, you're all right." And when that doctor started quoting him numbers about his odds for living, it was like Karlen wasn't even there in the same room with him—as if Karlen was already back at the plant, already home.

He came back to work using that stub like a tool, and he was able to work pretty well that way. He even stopped a high-pressure spew-out on the Unit One reactor single-handed and got probably a half-year's dose of radiation to boot, all in about five minutes. He's a team player though—he flushed his exposure badge down the toilet and instead turned in a cool one to Buck, the radiation safety officer, saying some wisecrack about frying his eggs or something or other, and Buck just laughed. It was as though Karlen wanted real bad for us to think everything was the same as always. There he was grinning and joking just like before, as if to say, "Here I am, I'm still Karlen, I'm still the center of things—minus one arm that's all."

When he got sick again it was like it happened overnight. It happened right when the Unit Two reactor went on-line, after we'd all been working on it for eleven years. He went home that weekend and just stayed there. All of a sudden he sort of shriveled up, and I wasn't really all that surprised, as if somehow I knew it would happen, no matter what. And it was like Karlen knew it too—like he had known it for years, as if there had come a time in his life, years ago, when it had dawned on him, but by then it was too late to avoid it because, by then, his job was his life. And that's the truth, too— his job was his life, it was *him*, and now it was as if there was nothing he could do except believe, and have faith, and go on trying to live his life the way he always had lived it, no matter what—and to hell with guesswork about the future. Anyway, he got really bad. Aunt Maggie took care of him, but he didn't last much longer.

■

She kept his hair in a Wonder Bread bag, the teeth in a bouillon-cube jar. I saw them one Saturday morning, stored on the back porch shelf where Karlen keeps his fishing tackle, right next to Maggie's big canning-kettle. The reason I was there was, I still didn't know how bad he was, and early that morning he'd called me to go fishing like it was no big deal. And I guess he didn't know how bad he was either, even with his arm cut off and his teeth falling out. So there I was sitting on his back porch waiting for him. I always waited outside like that on hunting or fishing days, I guess because of Maggie, I don't know—like there was this line I shouldn't step across if it was just fishing. I could hear squirrels scuttling across the tin porch roof right above my head and there was these purplish blackbirds pecking around in the backyard grass. Then the birds jumped into the sky and flew over the chain-link fence down toward the graveyard, and I got up, too, and went over to the shelf to get down the tackle box, and that's when the bouillon-cube jar caught my eye. I reached for it and held it up into a beam of sunshine, and there were these teeth in it. The light sort of passed through them and made them glow out at me. There were about twelve of them, some with little dots of dried blood. I'm thinking, "Human," and right then I hear some rattling behind me at the kitchen door and I look up and see Maggie's gray face in the door window. She's fiddling around with the chain on the inside of the door, and she's already hollering at me. So I look off into the grass and turn off the sound, and then I hold the jar up in the sunshine again and look at it even though I can feel her eyes jabbing out at me right through that door. And right then I see this short little guy in a white lab coat. He's walking across the grass like he'd always been walking across the grass. He's walking across the grass like he owned the grass. He had his arm sticking toward me and his face was grinning and his mouth was talking and he was like a walking, talking, rubber-mouth doll, and I just stayed real still and quiet, staring at him, trying not to tell him anything with my face. And then his grin floats away and his face clouds up and he reaches for the jar, looking at it with his hard pink eyes and a scrunched forehead that's like part of his eyes, and I jerk the jar back away from him, not knowing exactly why, and I feel Maggie at my side, and

24

she's shooing the guy away, like shooing away flies with the back of her hand. So he leaves. Then I feel her cold hands pry my fingers off the jar, and she takes it and drops it down inside the Wonder Bread bag. She throws the bag into the kettle on the porch shelf, and everything is as silent as snowflakes falling. Then she goes back through the door and slams it, and through the glass I see Karlen for the last time ever. He's standing there smiling—a wide, squashed, red-gum smile with his face thin and pale like steam, and he winks and waves at me, with a nod of his head. He waves at me and nods, and Maggie takes him away. I tried the door but it wouldn't open, and it was like he was still winking at me. A big pot of something was boiling on the kitchen stove. I sat down on the porch a while longer, waiting, and finally I walked to the river alone.

■

Four weeks later Karlen O'Malley was dead. In the plant lunchroom the day of his funeral, that same white-coat guy I'd seen on Karlen's back porch sat down next to me and stuck his hand out, talking and smiling real big. By then I knew all about him. He was the rad-guy, the new radiation safety officer, a real knock-'em-dead scientist-type sent down from D.C. They gave Buck a nice desk job downtown and sent this guy in to take his place. It was Karlen himself who told me, in one of several phone calls he made to me in his last days. Karlen would call to chat about this or that, like it was an ordinary thing to do and everything was just normal and fine—even though he was calling from his very deathbed, it turns out.

Karlen said this new guy was a regulation-book puppet—a walking, talking lawsuit shield. And sure enough, he spewed out memos like steam from a busted pipe. He always wore that white lab coat and that black tie like some hotshot, and nobody at the plant liked him, especially me. And there he was in the lunchroom, holding out his pink hand to me and running his blame mouth. I had my sound off, and I sat there eating some boiled okra and watching his talking mouth and gummy white grin, and I thought, "To hell with his lab coat and his necktie, I'm *keeping* the sound off." I sat there eating that okra and looking at his hand until he dropped it, and then I stared straight at him, trying not to blink. His words were like tiny squeaks and his mouth kept moving and finally stopped, and his grin went away. He looked down at the dead trout on his plate and started nibbling at it a little, and after a while he got up and left, kind of frowning. Screw him. He'd been messing around, bugging people about whatever he's paid to bug people about. Even with Karlen on his deathbed this guy had just dropped in right out of the blue with that big car-salesman grin and started telling Karlen how tragic it was, but there was no scientific proof his illness was caused by working at the plant—as if he was afraid Karlen might make the government pay the hundred-dollar deductible on his health insurance, or something. Screw him, smiles or no smiles, necktie or no necktie.

Then about an hour before quitting time he comes back up to me while I'm mopping up around Unit Two. I have on one of those little white suits you always have to wear when you're inside the containment building, and here comes the rad-guy with his lab coat and his necktie, and there's Ron the supervisor behind him with his necktie, too. Ron's giving me his stop-this-shit look, so I figure I'll have to turn the sound on. I reach behind my ear and tune in what the rad-guy is saying. For once he isn't smiling. He says, "You some kind of idiot or something?" and I nod my head. I run my fingers along the mop handle and look down and see light shining off his shoes. Then he says, "This time it's point-blank, no shitting around—who's got the teeth?" I look at him and then over at Ron the supervisor. Ron's face says, Sorry, man, sorry, and then Ron's mouth says, "They can run tests on them, you know. Strontium 90 and all that. It's a new kind of thing." I shrug my shoulders and say, "What for?" and they both stare at me like stone faces. Then the rad-guy says, "The powers that be" in his best smart-ass voice, and I think, Yeah, that's right, we all got to cover our asses. I look down at the mop water for a while and then I say, "I ain't got them." So the rad-guy says, "Well then, who does?"

So I'm standing there thinking, "Hell, they're probably fertilizer by now. They're boiled, ground up, spread out like mayonnaise." I dip my mop down in the bucket and the light in the bucket breaks up into a million little pieces. I squeeze the mop and flop it on the floor and look up at the rad-guy. Then I look at Ron the supervisor and he looks sick, like a pale avocado. I lean the mop handle against my shoulder and reach up behind my ear with one hand and scratch my butt with the other.

"You like tomatoes?" I say. I look at the rad-guy. The two neckties look at each other and then back at me and I'm stone-faced. I mop awhile, feeling real nervous. They mutter to each other awhile, and finally they walk away. I walk away, too. I leave the mop and bucket and walk through the gate past the guard shack, still wearing my little white radiation suit and not giving a damn. The giant hourglass cooling towers are like tombstones, throwing long shadows across the ground, and I walk on a path that takes me the back way along the river, thinking I should've gone to that funeral.

■

So I walked along the river to Karlen's yard, still wearing my radiation suit. I turned the sound on and leaned up against that chain-link and everything was quiet. Maggie was stooped on the other side of the fence behind me, working in the garden as if she hadn't left it all day, except now she wore a black dress like widows do. The evening sun was behind me, covered by some clouds, but it shone through just enough to make my shadow, and then Maggie's shadow came up beside it. There was that chain-link shadow and both of our shadows on it, flattened out and pointing toward the graveyard, and I leaned there looking down the slope of the hill at the filled-in hole they'd finally dug for Karlen in the ground, with flowers piled on top of it. It was near where the stump was, as if he was a seed. I could see Maggie's tin potion bucket sitting on the grass by the flowers. Without the big ash tree, the sky stood out plain and smooth like a bright bowl, not broken by grids and webs of limbs the way it had been for a hundred years, and Maggie's head shadow leaned toward me and said, "He willed you his truck and some pictures of General MacArthur." I didn't say anything, and then her body shadow got bigger. "And these, what's left of 'em." Her hand shadow moved up, with a shadow of something dangling from it—a bag or something.

I looked at that bag shadow, knowing it was Karlen's teeth and wondering what Karlen would do if he was me. And then all of a sudden I didn't give a damn what he would do. I said, "You know, we could prove what killed him with those teeth. Scientific proof." Then we were both quiet a while. And I was thinking, "Of course, that would do Karlen a hell of a lot of good. Might as well plant them and hope they'll sprout, for all the good it'll do Karlen." Then I said, "But I wonder if we can trust the bastards," and Maggie laughed, quick and sharp, an accusing kind of laugh—as if trust was the craziest thing in the world, a stupid thing to even think about. I stared at our shadows for a while, the empty graveyard.

White sawdust lay scattered across the graves. In silence I watched Maggie's hand shadow disappear, and the bag shadow disappeared with it, hiding inside her body shadow. Then Maggie started singing, softly. I couldn't quite make out the words, and I didn't like the funny way it sounded, so I turned off the sound. Then she went away.

The wind was blowing and for a while I leaned there on the chain-link in the silent wind. After a while I turned around toward Maggie's garden, and she was on her knees, digging in the dirt with the hand trowel. That D.C. rad-guy was standing beside her with sadness spread over his face like sweat, a sad mask of sweat. He was looking at Maggie like looking at some kind of museum, some kind of exhibit growing in a tomato patch inside a terrarium, and Maggie looked up at him with eyes like needles sticking in a doll. He was saying something to her. His face gnarled close around his lips while the flaps of skin under his eyes pushed up, making his eyes look pained and distant and urgent with importance and hope, the way greed is. Maggie stood up and looked straight at him.

He kept talking and I'm thinking, "Turn on the sound," so I start messing with it and sounds get all mixed up together. His words get mixed in with a chattering squirrel and with the wind blowing through the trees. So I turn off the sound and his face is still working, and for a long time it just goes on that way and all I can hear is a tiny squeaking noise coming from him, like a hinge. Maggie just stands there the way walls just stand there and say, "Looky here, a wall."

Finally he does it—he sheds his sadness-face, just crawls out of it. He's turned just plain mad, mad at Maggie standing there in her widow dress, mad at me standing there in my white radiation suit, and his face is orange in the long light. Then he stops short and looks at me like throwing something at me, and he turns and walks away. Maggie walks to the edge of the garden and picks up the shovel. Her lips move like wooden toys, and she's looking at him. She's leaning on the shovel beside the red dirt, and she's looking at him. He stops at the road about fifty feet away beside his government car and turns to look back at her. Her arm curves up from the socket and bends at the elbow, beckoning him back. So he comes back.

The sun is wild and low and the sky screams out color and he stands there droop-faced with his black tie still black and his lab coat stained pink in the sun and his ID badge clipped to his lapel with his rubbery face grinning on it, and she holds the shovel out to him. He folds his fingers around the worn wooden handle and runs his eyes along it to the garden dirt. Maggie's dress is deep black and she steps back a couple of steps and grins at him. I can see the Wonder Bread bag behind him, blowing empty across the grass. Maggie turns to me and grins real big. Karlen's not a hundred yards away in his grave, and she stands there in a tomato patch and grins real big like that.

■

I can imagine how it must've been in his last days. Maggie would've been on her knees, shuffling through the tissue paper in the bathroom wastebasket, picking out teeth and hunks of that stuck-together hair, but Karlen wouldn't notice because he'd be puking into a plastic can in the bedroom, dying that way. Slow and fluid, ounce by ounce, alone in that dark room with only Maggie floating through ever now and then with a broom, or with one of her magic potions to rub on him or pour down his throat. It doesn't seem natural and I don't like to think of it—him dying that way in that room. I'd rather imagine him digging a field line, say, or tinkering with his pickup— dropping the clutch or transmission or something. He'd have his arm back somehow, as though Maggie might've sewed on a new one, and he'd be laying in gravel under the truck, and the truck would be full of George Jones and Tammy Wynette, the long strands of music filling the cab and leaking through the windows like it always did those mornings I rode with him to work. I can imagine him on his back in that gravel, singing those songs about whiskey and hard times, flipping his long bloody teeth from his fingers like cigarette butts, or spitting them into the gravel beside him, spitting them like grape seeds or lumps of tobacco, his cheeks flushed bright red and his eyes dancing—even the fleshy tops of his fingers looking red like apples in the cold air. It would be the hard clear air of autumn, the kind that moves around a lot and chills the surface of your skin. He would lie in that crushed limestone and loosen those rusty bolts, cursing them until they creaked open, then singing again as he worked the wrench. The truck would sway gently as he worked the wrench. His hair would float from his head, loosening and taking off, hunks of it drifting from under that pickup and rising on the breeze like cattail seed into blue air. He'd be falling apart piece by piece but he'd say, "Fine, no problem, everything's fine." He'd just grin and fart and turn the ratchet, maybe with some transmission fluid streaming down his arms, and him too busy to worry with a few loose teeth. He'd say to hell with it. To hell with those teeth and that hair, so long as it floats away from him, doesn't get in his way. He wouldn't notice Maggie, quiet and tiny, gathering those teeth into her dry, spotted hands and clutching them to her breast. He'd be too busy. Too busy to drop the ratchet and get up from the gravel and dust off his lime-white clothes and have a cup of herbal tea. Too busy to let his body give out until the job is done. Too busy to stop grinning, even for a moment, and look straight on at things that really can't be seen—things invisible and deadly in a creeping way, things hiding and floating and shining in the cold air around him.

Home for the Weekend

The sun played tricks on our eyes. The trees and grass and weeds and even Mrs. Maplethorne's Pepto-pink house and plastic flamingos seemed cooled-off and faded, and the colors of everything we passed seemed cooler and dimmer and faded the way old jeans get faded. Steve's bike had a transistor radio on the handlebars. It played Jet-Fly WFLI, the rock station out of Chattanooga, with a deejay who called himself Chickamauga Charlie, the Motor Mouth of the Mid-South—who my drunk Uncle Newt said was a carpetbagger—but it didn't come in real clear. The beat came through okay, though. Steve's favorite group was the Beatles, and Steve's parents even let him have a Beatles' haircut. I liked the Beatles, too, and Little Stevie Wonder and Jefferson Airplane and the Rolling Stones.

We were riding to Winkler's store, out past the church. Tar was bubbling up in big splotches on the road, and the honeysuckle smelled like it was frying, or maybe that was the tar smell mixed in. Sometimes gravel stuck to our tires and slung off, pinging through the spokes and knocking us in the back of our heads. When we got to the church Steve rode past me, heading for shade. His shirt was wrapped around his waist, dragging a little on the rear wheel, and his back was shiny with sweat. His bike had gooseneck handlebars and a banana seat with purple glitter in it, and he could pop wheelies. My bike was a plain one that wouldn't pop wheelies. Steve didn't have to go to church on Sunday like me, but we did lots of other stuff together.

I decided to cut into the empty church lot and coast across the blacktop. I did a couple of loops and hit some speed bumps and then stopped at the place where the blacktop met the road. Steve was gone now into the trees, and the radio sound was gone, and there was just the sound of me breathing and some crows cawing across the road, hidden in the leaves of the old pear tree we thought was dead last fall. I looked down at a grasshopper caught in a patch of tar. It wiggled a while and then stopped, and I got my energy up and pulled onto the road, and I could see the tire marks where Mr. Thrasher laid tracks the Sunday before with his GMC pickup because Qunu, the African guy, was sitting in church like he belonged there, where no black person had ever been before in history, it turns out.

The tire tracks went in and out of tar puddles and ended where the road ducked into the shade. The shade seemed dark like a basement, and I saw Steve a ways off, pedaling hard in the shadows. Really it had only been three days since Old Man Thrasher drove away mad from church, but it seemed longer somehow. And it's funny how he peeled away crazy like that, not knowing half the congregation walked out after him. They walked out during the "Onward Christian Soldiers" song. Qunu—who my big brother Mike brought home from college for the weekend—just sat drowsy and smiling on the pew, like he didn't even know what was going on around him. I'll never forget the look on Mr. Thrasher's meaty face, and his thin white hair, even whiter next to his face, and that pulsing in his temples as he steamed down the aisle toward the door, looking red in the face the way I figured me and Steve looked now, sweating up the hill on our bikes in the heat. That was the last time I ever saw Thrasher dead or alive, and I wasn't surprised when they said his soul had already departed before his pickup ever crashed into Soddy Creek. I knew that about him, how he got mad over things.

It didn't seem cool in the shade. My shirt stuck to me and my eyes were stinging from sweat. I saw Steve ahead of me, about halfway up the big hill, starting to tire out. Winkler's store was on the other side of the hill. I had some money in my pocket, money Mr. Thrasher paid me Saturday, the day before he died. It was for helping him cut down the "Eat at Stuckey's" sign they put in his pasture near the I-24 off-ramp by mistake. Me and Steve probably wouldn't have been riding to Winkler's if it hadn't been for the extra money I made off old Thrasher. Steve stood waiting for me beside the speed limit sign halfway up the hill. The shade seemed dark and close like in a movie house, and Steve was gesturing for me, yelling "Hurry Ian, hurry." He needed me because he had spent all his money on a Jimi Hendrix black-light poster and the new Rolling Stones album, and he never worked like me anyway.

Mr. Thrasher always said work is what makes men men, but that kind of crap was crap and I knew it. I just wanted money, but I never said anything to make him think different. I had showed up early that morning we cut down the Stuckey's sign, and I heard him cussing to his wife about car fumes from the new Interstate blowing across his farm, and about those damn fools from Stuckey's, and he cussed on and on and on because he didn't know yet that I was there—him the head of the deacons and me a church youth to make an example for, and him cussing as bad as my drunk Army uncle.

35

Steve, he had a rich daddy who treated him like he was something special, buying him that fancy bike and giving him an allowance and all. I reckon Steve thought I should treat him the same way, because there he was at the speed limit sign, combing his sweaty Beatle hair and expecting me to hurry so we could buy Cokes with money I made off Old Man Thrasher. My guess was Mr. Thrasher felt bad about that cussing, so he tried to make up for it by acting goofy all day and throwing his money around. When we got finished sawing down that sign, we dragged it to his house with the tractor and broke it up with a sledgehammer and used the wood to make a doghouse and a picnic table for his patio, and he cut out the wood just right so that the Stuckey's Pecan Log was on top of the picnic table, and he thought that was so clever he called his wife out to see, which wasn't like him. Then he gave me $2.00 per hour instead of $1.50 without me asking, which wasn't like him either. So I guess I profited from his cussing, but stood to lose from his dying, since he had lots of jobs lined up which I couldn't possibly do with him dead.

I raced Steve down the hill to Winkler's and I won, even though his bike was brand new and fancy, which is proof that how things look ain't always the main thing. Mr. Winkler was sitting on the bench beside the kerosene pump. He had his britches pulled up above his navel and a chew of tobacco, and his nose had a red sore on it. He said, "Don't let your pinkie stick out like that." I grinned but didn't say anything, and Steve just walked right into the store, so I did too. It smelled like bubble gum in there, and a big fan was blowing, and the radio was playing some kind of march music. We both got a Dr Pepper out of the drink box, and peanuts, and when nobody was looking, I got some Double Bubble and stuck it in my pocket. Mr. Winkler's *Chattanooga Times* newspaper was on the counter. It was all wrinkled and had something sticky on it. "What you doing, Ian?" said Steve, and I said I was looking to see who's winning the war, stupid. I always did that. I would scan the articles out of Saigon and find the tallies, usually at the end of the story, and today it turned out, like most days, that more Cong were killed than Americans—thirty-two Cong to seventeen Americans. Then I checked the sports page to see if Hank Aaron hit any home runs in the St. Louis game, but he didn't. He was 0 for 4. Steve said, "When I get there I want to fly a bomber or a helicopter, one of those big Huey gunships." He held his arms out and made a machine gun noise.

Mr. Winkler came in kind of limping from his bad war knee and said, "How's your brother doing?" I knew he wasn't really asking that, though, because what he really wanted to know was, "What's going on with this Nigra-in-the-church business?" Mr. Winkler used to be my Sunday School teacher, and he taught me a long time ago never to say nigger. He said "Nigra" instead, with an "uh" sound at the end, like "bazooka." My brother Mike, who's going to be a preacher, says Negro with an O. I figured it didn't much matter so long as you treated everybody the same, but what about Qunu, the African guy? Did they treat him the same? I wondered if it would have made any difference if Old Man Thrasher had known Qunu was a foreigner, from Africa, instead of some guy from 9th Street in downtown Chattanooga, which was probably where everybody thought he was from. What they didn't know was, Qunu was from Nigeria, and my brother Mike met him at college in Nashville and converted him and brought him home for the weekend, which is what Jesus would do, and I believe that. Jesus himself had long hair and a beard, but that didn't mean he was a bad person. What matters is inside. Even Old Man Thrasher once told me what matters is inside. What he said was, "Clothes don't make the man," and that's the same thing.

Mr. Winkler was smiling that tobacco-bump smile and ringing up

37

our Dr Peppers and peanuts and hoping I would say if Qunu was coming back next Sunday or not. Steve wanted me to buy him some baseball cards. He promised he would pay me back and I said okay, but if there's a Hank Aaron or Rico Carty it was mine, so he said forget it, and I said, okay then, forget it.

The radio behind Mr. Winkler's head was talking about the riots. They still had downtown Chattanooga closed off. The black folks there were really mad about stuff like garbage and low wages and bad plumbing and equal rights. The radio said it was really hot downtown, and that made it worse. It said people get crazy when it's hot. Then it switched to an Aqua Velva commercial. I said if they're so hot they may as well go swimming instead of having riots, and Mr. Winkler said they ought to shoot every last one of them. Then he asked whether Mike's old Dodge Dart car was still working, and I said it was. Last summer Mike helped Mr. Winkler paint the store white with blue trim and then bought the car with the money, but Mr. Winkler was so impressed he acted like Mike did it for free or something and then built the car with his own hands. Mike was a born leader. He got to preach sometimes at his college church and he had a new mustache, which was unusual for a preacher. He thought a mustache might help him convert hippies or something, so it worked kind of like a disguise. That's how Mike is. Sometimes it seemed he'd never done nothing wrong in his whole life, but of course that's not true of anybody human. One time a big rain was washing away the pavement at the end of our driveway because the drainpipe was clogged, so Mike, who was in junior high then, went out in the rain with the flat-nose shovel without anybody making him and unclogged the drain and saved the driveway. I wished I had thought of unclogging that drain. I heard Daddy bragging to Tom Sands, his buddy from work, about Mike doing that all on his own, and he talked on and on about it, so I hid in my room and made noises into the big window fan and wouldn't come out to supper.

I paid for the Dr Peppers and peanuts with dimes and nickels and pennies, and Mr. Winkler spread them out on the counter and grouped them by type and counted in a whisper to himself. He always counted real slow and careful like that. He liked Mike, and he liked me too, but he liked me more in the way you like something that reminds you of yourself, not the way you like somebody because you know he's something you can't be, which is how he liked Mike. Mr. Winkler was always full of surprises. Sometimes he said things I thought an adult, especially a church adult, would never say. Once, a while back, when we still lived out this way, he told me how sex works—the how-to details of it. He told it to me one morning when I was waiting for the school bus at his store during a cold rain, and I told him he was crazy, so he stood there grinning, thinking it was funny that I didn't believe a word he said.

I put my Dr Pepper bottle in the empties rack and stood by the door waiting for him to finish counting my money, but after a while I shrugged and said, "Come on, Steve, we gotta get going." The screen door made a long whangy sound, and Mr. Winkler looked up from the counter and said, "Hey!" We both stopped and he said, "Don't let your pinkies stick out," and Steve said, "What?" He said, "You know what a pinkie is don't you?" and Steve held up his little finger and looked at it, and Winkler said, "No, it's your pecker." He said that's what they called peckers when he was in the Army. He grinned when he said it. He always grinned instead of laughing. Steve laughed, but I just let the screen door swing shut behind me. I hate the way people play around with words that way. I went over to Steve's bike and turned on the radio, but it was so garbled I turned it off.

The heat seemed worse when we pedaled away from the store

with all that Dr Pepper fizz in our bellies. We decided to head for the lake and I took off real fast, like we were racing. Steve passed me at Thrasher Hill, where a dirt road cuts off to the old cemetery. He had his shirt tied around his waist, and his hair was blowing and his shirt was flopping, and he had on dark sunglasses. He laughed and waved back at me and pointed to the glasses, and I knew right off he stole them from Winkler's.

I slowed my bike in the cool shade, coasting down the hill to where the oak and hickory woods gave way to rows of tall pines. I got off my bike and watched Steve ride away. He seemed to disappear when he rode through patches of sunshine. At the crest of the next hill he looked back, and I leaned my bike in the ditch and headed off through the pines toward the river.

The pines were in neat rows the way they'd been planted thirty years ago when the dam was built and the valley got flooded. My drunk uncle, Uncle Newt, told me crews of black men planted the trees as part of a government make-work plan, but I know my own grandfather planted some too, because my grandmother said so, but my drunk uncle says no he didn't either, he just helped with some dredging and clearing in the valley, which was the government make-work plan for whites. I walked on the brown needles under the pines and came to the water's edge, and Steve came up behind me and said, "There ain't no swimming here," so I told him I was tired of swimming in this stinking river anyway. Steve clapped at a mosquito in the air and we could hear the pop of his hands echo across the water. The water smelled like dead fish and there was no wind moving through the hot air.

I'd forgotton about the cemetery. I could see it across the slough. It was the old church cemetery, gray with headstones and big graveyard oaks. The oaks stood tall above the pine rows like an island, the big upper limbs a tangle of deadwood and pale green. For the first time I could remember, the graveyard was weeded and mowed and looked almost neat. A green awning was pitched beside a bright pile of red earth. A row of flowers on metal stands stood beside the dirt. I figured it was for Old Man Thrasher.

Old Man Thrasher. I caught an eight-pound largemouth bass in this slough once, or maybe in a different slough just like it on the other side of the hill, I'm not sure. I'm not sure because we came in Thrasher's bass boat instead of by land. Sometimes when you come at something from a slightly different angle you might not recognize it—even if it's the place where you grew up and know like the back of your hand.

But I do remember we were somewhere near the cemetery when I caught that eight-pounder. We had arrived just after dawn, and I sat watching Mr. Thrasher cast a top lure, jerking it across the mucky green water. He talked about church as he fished. He said the original church—the one that our church came from, the one which his granddaddy was preacher in—was originally where the slough is now, the one we were fishing in. Maybe it was down beneath us somewhere. When he said it I was tying on a plastic worm the way he'd showed me, and I looked across the water, flat and smooth and dark, and I tried to imagine the church under there. Maybe bluegill swam in the baptistry. Maybe a turtle peered down from the pulpit.

Then Mr. Thrasher let his line lay still for a while. He stopped talking and slapped at some gnats in front of his eyes and pulled his glasses off and put them back on again, already sweating in the still, morning air. His line stretched some thirty feet across the slough, and the lure floated, motionless. Mr. Thrasher looked up at the sky for a moment and then leaned down to the minnow bucket, thinking maybe he should try one of the live ones instead of the plastic jitterbug he was using, and right then, right when he stuck his hand in the minnow bucket and kind of splashed around in it, with his line stretched out small and still and quiet, and with him grunting a little and breathing hard as he bent to check the minnow bucket, right then, when he wasn't even thinking about it, he got a hit—and it was a hard one. The fish broke water and Thrasher stood quick and the bass boat rocked and there was splashing in the water and then it was gone, so he let out some line and it whirred out fast from the reel, and he stood in the swaying boat while the line whined from the reel and then slowed, and finally he added some drag and his rod bent double and in no time that fish wrapped around something deep in the water and snapped his twelve-pound-test line like taffy. Right then I thought of church steps rising to nowhere out of the muck and that fish, desperate, doing all it could do.

I squatted beside the slough and looked across at Thrasher's new grave and wondered if Steve thought we shouldn't swim here because of that, because of whatever was hidden at the bottom of the slough, deep in the silt there. But after a few minutes he said he was going swimming after all. He set his stolen sunglasses on a rock, dropped his clothes, and jumped all the way under. I got a stick and started digging in the red mud at the edge of the water. In a minute he bobbed up with his hair stuck to his head like a painted-on helmet and said he'd like to take a gunboat up the Mekong River and blast gooks out of the trees. Then he dove back under and bobbed up a few feet away and said he'd like to be a sharpshooter. He thought he was a big warrior because his uncle bought him a pellet gun for his birthday, and his father's grandfather was a sharpshooter under General Longstreet in the Battle of Chickamauga. I told him my brother Mike was a sharpshooter in ROTC at college. I'd seen his targets he brought home, with grades from the teacher, and he got mostly A's and A-minuses and lots of the bull's-eyes were shot out. ROTC was what he had to do because he got out of the draft because he was going to be a preacher.

I wondered how it would be if Mike had gone to Vietnam instead of college. Would he have brought home some Vietnamese guy? And would the church split up over that the way it did over Qunu, the African guy? The first time Qunu came to our house he laid in our living room and watched TV. He was wearing some of Mike's old cutoff shorts that Momma had been saving for me, but Qunu needed them now. He laid there watching *Hee-Haw* and laughing till tears rolled down his cheeks. He had tribal marks on his cheeks, where they cut him to show he's a man. Up until *Hee-Haw* came on he'd been real quiet, so it seemed strange to see him laugh so hard, and afterward he got real quiet again. Qunu didn't have any money or anything, being from Nigeria, and that's why we were trying to help him. Mike thought the church would help too, since, after all, he had converted him and Qunu was a Christian now. But as it turned out, things just aren't that simple. Some people pitched in— folks like the Overstreets, Steve's daddy, even Mr. Winkler—but others didn't. I watched Steve, floating now on his back in a streak of gold light reflecting off the slough-water. He was talking about quail hunting and wishing he could have a new shotgun. I squinted at him a while and then picked up those stolen sunglasses he'd left on the rock. They still had the price tag on them, with Mr. Winkler's "7.95" in real shaky writing. I held the glasses up against the sky at arm's length and looked through the dark lenses, at the coolness in them. Right then I started thinking that maybe Qunu got himself converted for no good reason. I liked *Hee-Haw* but I never thought it was all *that* funny, and sometimes I think he was laughing at every-thing, not just the jokes that were supposed to be funny. He even laughed at the commercials and sometimes Walter Cronkite. Didn't

Mr. Thrasher say that black folks just sing and dance at church, instead of having real church like us? Then I remembered Qunu sitting on the pew that morning, kind of sleepy and smiling but real quiet and still, and I just didn't know. I watched Steve float around like a dead log and I slapped at mosquitoes and wished I was old enough to go off to college right now. I got a piece of bubble gum from my pocket, soft and warm, and bit into it. I swallowed the sweet juice and wondered if someday I would find a Nigerian to bring home for the weekend. I thought about old Mrs. Maplethorne, how she called up my momma on the phone and said if she was twenty years younger she'd come over and break every bone in Momma's body because she let Mike bring Qunu to church. Momma didn't care; she sounded real proud of Mike and told old Maplethorne to take her Geritol and come on, she's ready for her.

Steve stood over me as white as a sheet. I squatted there in the red mud staring up at him dripping in the sun, and he asked me what's wrong. I said Old Man Thrasher's dead and it looks like they're fixing to bury him over across the slough sometime later today. He squatted down dripping beside me and rained lake water on some ants that were dragging away a dead grasshopper and said, "Oh, that old fart." It didn't seem right, but I went ahead and said, "Yeah, that old fart." I told Steve how Old Man Thrasher got so mad his blood pressure went up and he just dropped dead, and how the church split up too. While I spoke we watched a big mud turtle stick its head up a few feet away and sort of look at us before diving back under water. We could see its shell covered with layers of mud and pebbles, and right then Steve turned to me, frowning in the sun, and said, "Why?" I looked at him like he had asked some real important question that went to the core of the fight, the inside guts of it. I thought he really was on to it. The way he asked "Why?" made it sound like, just for a second, he was questioning the truth about it. But then I wasn't so sure. It could be that he just didn't know. Maybe he said "Why" that way because he just didn't know, because he didn't go to church and didn't know the problem and couldn't know. Maybe what we think of as really smart questions are questions that are asked because we don't know any better. Maybe we're all just ignorant. I looked at Steve's pale face, his flat belly, his legs folded under him as he squatted there beside me. Ants were crawling up his ankles, dodging the drops of river water running down his skin. He looked out at the slough. I looked down at the red mud, the oozy lip of the green shiny water.

It was too hot. I stood up and put my hands above my eyes and looked at the sky, which still didn't have any clouds in it, but wasn't exactly blue either. I stooped low at the silent edge of the sun-filled slough and scooped some of that dark water in my hands, clear in my palms, and spread it across my face. It felt hot and clung to my skin. Steve stood up quick and ran into the water, jumped all the way under in one quick move. I turned and started back through the pines before he came up for air.

A Few Casualties

I worked for Roy Winkler's daddy, when I was about fifteen or sixteen, doing odd jobs while Mr. Winkler kept the store. He had horses and an old pecan grove not far from our place. In autumn I gathered pecans and put them in brown paper bags to sell in the store. In the summers I mowed the grass around his house with an old push-mower. Afterward I would walk through the pecan grove down to Winkler's dock by the river and dive in naked, my hands numb from the mowing, my body covered with sweat. Sometimes I would dig worms from the black earth near the riverbank and put them in a coffee can, and I would borrow the Winklers' johnboat and fish for bluegill, floating with the current in the sun, watching the red-and-white bobber drift across swirls of dark water.

Roy was there, that first summer I worked for Mr. Winkler. He was no good, Mr. Winkler told me: his son Roy was worthless. I remember the quiver in his lips when he said it, the way his eyes shrunk from mine. "Now Victor, don't you grow up to be like Roy," he would say, and he really seemed to worry about it.

But I was fascinated by Roy. When I first began working there, Roy had just graduated from high school, so he didn't have anything to do. He would drive his Harley around like a madman, or else he would lie in his room smoking cigarettes all day. Sometimes I would see him on the lawn or on the porch, holding a transistor radio to his ear, eyes closed, swaying slightly. His bedroom was plastered with pictures of Elvis Presley and the Beatles. He wore black jeans and a black leather jacket. He had long sideburns, and his hair was long and straight like John Lennon's.

He was dating Mary Liz Barter that summer, and everybody knew about them. Mary Liz had thick red lips and cottony skin that turned red in the sun, and she kept her red hair stacked high on her head. Somehow her hair wouldn't blow free, even when Roy doubled her on his Harley.

Sometimes I would sneak through the foliage down to the river. I would crouch in the willows and oaks beside the water and watch Mary Liz and Roy on the dock, stretched out on orange beach towels in the heat. Roy wore purple striped trunks, and Mary Liz had a red bikini. They listened to rock music on the transistor radio, lying still and breathless like photos from a magazine. Now and then they would touch and kiss. I heard their giggles, and sometimes I saw them naked, too, wrapped tight together on the gray worn dock in the empty cove. Mary Liz might tickle him and laugh, her breasts jiggling as she rose to her feet, her shoulders and belly red from the sun. She would dive off the dock, her body snapping long and tight in the thick air above the water, stabbing into it like an arrow, and Roy would follow, cursing, his muscles taut across his shoulders, his chest pumped up with air. They would caress in the water, bobbing nose to nose, two heads floating above the green murk of the river.

He bought me off with comic books and Coca-Cola. He gave me

gasoline for the johnboat and let me borrow his Zebco reel and fiber-glass rod, and all I had to do was keep quiet about Mary Liz, as if I knew a secret nobody else knew. One August afternoon he let me shoot squirrels with his shotgun, blasting them out of the trees where they hoarded pecans in big gray nests. He showed me how to hold the gun and aim, how to keep the gun steady while pulling the trigger. I saw his biceps quiver with each blast, his skin as smooth and clean as the worn walnut gunstock. He gave me the gun and stood behind me, stretching his arms around me to help position it. He was quiet and patient and larger than life: Sergeant Murphy attacking Hamburger Hill; Tarzan, Superman, Captain Marvel. I shot down whole limbs, showering the ground with leaves and green pecans.

I lay in bed those summer nights, running my hands across my skin in the darkness, thinking of Mary Liz: the way her shoulders moved when she laughed; the way sunlight seemed to twine around her, holding her high and weightless in space; the way her body hovered and turned above the water. I tried to imagine how I might look if I were beside her on the dock. I imagined peeling off Roy's skin, slipping into it like slipping into a pair of overalls, using it as a disguise: his smooth shoulders, his gentle face.

By the next summer—my second and last summer working at Winkler's—Roy and Mary Liz had broken up. Roy was in basic training at Ft. Bragg, North Carolina, and Mary Liz moved to Atlanta to live with her sister. Roy took two tours of duty in Vietnam while I was in high school. He was a volunteer.

■

Mr. Winkler kept an old mare named Suey in a pasture near the pecan grove. Suey was my daddy's horse, the one Momma let Mr. Winkler have when Daddy died in Vietnam. Momma had let Daddy keep horses on our farm, but she had little else to do with him after the divorce. He lived in a trailer several miles away, but he took good care of those horses, driving by the house every day on his way to the barn and then leaving without saying a word to us. One time he bought me a .22 rifle, but he couldn't bring himself to hand it to me—he just dropped it off on the front porch. I remember him as little more than hired help, really. When he went to the war, he hired a guy to take his place, and it didn't make much difference.

Once when I was pruning deadwood in Mr. Winkler's pecan grove I saw Suey emerge from the trees far across the pasture. She stood still in the open sun, facing me, and for a moment I thought she could actually see me. Despite the great distance, I imagined that I could see her eyes and that she could see mine. Then she disappeared into the shadow of the trees, suddenly, as though she had become frightened. That was the first time in years I had thought of my father. And it was the first and only time I cried for his loss.

■

My friend Bernie and I shared stories about the war and about people from our town who had gone to fight in it. Bernie lived with his father and his color TV in a three-room tar-paper shack set back in the woods beside an abandoned limestone quarry. When Bernie's old man was on day shift at the pencil factory or passed out drunk, we would sit at Bernie's house and read Combat comics and watch old war movies on their new color TV. Sometimes there would be news flashes about peace talks or astronauts or Russia or Vietnam, and when there were battlefield films out of Vietnam I watched closely, hoping through some miracle to catch a glimpse of Roy. I liked those battlefield films, the way the camera jerked and the artillery shells popped like tiny snapping twigs. It all seemed real, somehow, even though the color was often slightly shifted or washed out. The trees might be pastel green or banana yellow; soldier's wounds looked pink like carnations; and pale green soldiers walked to battle like bored students to history class: slow, measured, fumbling with chocolates and backpacks, plodding along like cattle. And then there were the black-and-white movies with Hollywood soldiers swaggering into battle, gray hunks of granite winning against all odds on some silver beach strewn with pale, dead, bloodless heroes. Bernie and I would sit on the sofa and smoke marijuana or sip warm beer and watch those films and talk about war, about what it looks like: about guns and planes and camps in the jungle. We invented women in that jungle, too, colorful and smiling and perfect, like something from a comic book. We were full of talk and hope, but we really didn't believe much of what we said. Somehow we did know this—our time would come. In whatever shape or form, we would have our war.

∎

The winter I turned eighteen was a long, silent winter. There was just me and Momma in the house, as usual, but for some reason the house seemed emptier than before. The silence between us was its own language: she sitting over her sewing, me with my schoolbooks, each avoiding the other's looks while the silence told us constantly of its presence. The weather grew unseasonably warm for a long while, and in February there was talk of bears breaking hibernation and roaming from the mountains to raid the farms. I had trouble sleeping then, too. In the dawn twilight I stood in the kitchen doorway looking across the backyard toward an old fencerow that was overgrown with weeds and cedars. I had seen something moving in the weeds there, something large and dark, and I stood in the open doorway with the shotgun, listening and looking intently at the fencerow.

The light was gray and slight, but I saw movement again and I heard some rustling. Then I saw a dark shape moving toward me. I put the gunstock against my shoulder and looked down the barrel as the shape moved up, stood erect, and stepped out of the weeds. My finger twitched but I held back and then lowered the barrel. It was Momma. In one hand she held a small trowel, and in the other an unopened daffodil—it was a bulb, actually, with dirt still clinging to it, sprouting a single bud. I watched silently as she crouched in the yard only a few feet from me, burying the bulb in the soil of a small clay pot. Beyond the fencerow I could see the gentle rise of our fields, overgrown with the husks of last year's milkweed and thistle. Off to the left were the old livestock pens, choked with weeds. And for a moment the sprout in that little pot seemed hideous, meant only to blot out a little more of what had once made this place a farm. Why did Momma want such a paltry thing? She patted the soil with the palm of her hand, smoothing it carefully. I stepped back through the doorway, still holding the shotgun. Momma looked up and saw me, but she didn't seem surprised. Her skin was the color of twilight. I put down the gun and turned away, running my hands across my chest. I could feel myself expanding, pushing through deep earth and through the decaying house itself, rising up to something she and I could not be sure of.

■

And when a kind of love came, I didn't tell Momma. On a cold day in March I picked up the telephone and heard a girl's voice—small, sweet, but not exactly timid—asking for someone named Lewis. I knew no one named Lewis. I said, "Lewis? Lewis? You want Lewis?" There was a pause and I could hear the quick whisper of her breath; then it stretched into a long sigh and she said, "Yes, I want Lewis. I said so, didn't I? Didn't I say I want Lewis?" So I said, "Yeah, well, maybe so, but to hell with Lewis. To hell with him." There was more silence after that, a bit longer this time, and I could feel cold sweat trickle on my skin. I had shocked myself with my own words, hardly able to believe that I would allow myself to speak that way to a girl. And then, just as I was about to hang up the phone, something happened that surpised me even more—she *giggled*. She giggled, then laughed. I laughed too, and we began to talk, and I fell in love.

It was just a voice I fell in love with, but I, too, was only a voice. We set up regular calls. Each evening I would lie on the upstairs sofa waiting for her, drawing in the smells of supper cooking in the kitchen below me. Old oak beams creaked heavily overhead, as though the empty spaces of that house were beginning to fill. She always called at the prearranged time; and when I begged to see her, she always refused. I could only bury my face under the dank cushions of the sofa, trying to imagine what she must be like: her skin moist, pale, layered like a pearl; her hair electric and shimmering in the air. Momma would yell from the bottom of the stairs: "That's enough now, we got a party line! And supper's ready, too. You hear?" But I floated alone and silent, out of body. "You hear me? You hear?"

She kept herself secret all that winter. I asked for pictures, but none came. She was just a voice flying across space: a kind of spirit. She was almost perfect. She called herself Shannon.

■

While Roy Winkler was away in Vietnam, his daddy went nuts. Nobody knew exactly why. It started when he got arrested for riding Suey through the produce section of the new supermarket on Highway 27. He was stark naked—all he wore was a Confederate soldier's cap, the kind they sell in souvenir shops—and he rode Suey in a slow plodding walk, around and around the vegetable bins, tipping that cap to the ladies and asking for directions to Kampuchea. He got so bad they finally had to lock him up in the County Home, a few weeks before Roy returned home. We learned later that the last months of Roy's two-year stint in the Army were spent stateside, in a hospital on the West Coast. He had suffered a serious wound to the chest, but he told no one the details of his injury—in fact, no one knew exactly when he returned to the empty house of the Winkler place. Suddenly he was just there.

I might have been one of the first people to know of Roy's return. One day in late January Roy picked up on the party line that we still shared with the Winklers, and he heard everything between me and Shannon. He just waited there and listened and finally said, in a raspy deep voice, "You about done? I gotta call the vet." Just like that, like the voice of God booming off Mount Sinai, just butting in to our private little dream like it was wired for sound, saying, "You done acted like a couple of animals who need a vet, so excuse me while I call one." For a moment the craziness of it hit me, both Shannon and me, and we muttered good-bye and fluttered back into the reality of our separate selves. Weeks passed before we spoke again.

■

Maybe Momma knew about the calls, too. One cold evening in April, Shannon called and Momma picked up on us. I heard the click from the downstairs extension. I felt sin; I felt a boundary crack. I started talking about Vietnam, as if I were talking to my friend Bernie. "When I get there," I said, "I'll eat rattlesnakes raw, I'll strip leaves from the jungle, I'll trample shallow graves." Shannon was silent, ethereal, transcendent. Momma said "Oops" and hung up, and I slammed down the phone. I ran out into the long evening light and trotted through a thin stand of pines to the bank of the river. I sat there on a fallen willow and watched the water for a while. It seemed to move as if it had a mission, as if it knew just what to do, and I watched it until the sun sputtered out. The sky blackened and deepened with tired old stars, and the breeze turned cold in the bare oaks at the riverbank. After a while I walked back toward the house, floating along in that kind of black whispering thickness you get on a moonless windy night under scraggly second-growth pines, and I could smell the smoke from Momma's fire before I could see the lights of the house. I took an armful of firewood from the woodshed and went in. Momma was asleep on the sofa near the fire. She was crumpled into a ball, covered with a quilt. I stood in the firelit room with an armful of wood and watched her for a long time. When the flame died down I added a log and walked quietly to my room.

■

In the days after she picked up the phone, Momma began looking at me in a new way, sending messages with her eyes. Finally the words came, too. It was as if she couldn't stand it anymore, as if something slipped inside her, and she had to transform her body to let words escape. I watched the whole thing: the roundness and depth of flesh and bone changed into color and line, into flatness, into cartoon. She became a cartoon and the words came out in clouds above her head, little word balloons. The first time it happened we were on the porch in a gray cool breeze, imagining warmth and sunshine the way you do in the first days of April when you've had enough of indoor winter air; the kind of air that bleeds from the pores of dead oak and sapless pine in the walls around you; the kind of air that you know you breathed yesterday and the day before and the day before that; the kind of air that you know someone else breathed before you,

55

some long-dead relative trapped in a dusty picture over the mantel or on the parlor wall. I sat on the porch with Momma, breathing the free air and listening for lost mockingbirds and smelling little exhalations of cornbread breath from the dark screen door behind us— hearing only the breathing of the house and the bony creaking of the timbers—and that's when the words came out. I read them in the air between us: "So tell me," she breathed. "Tell me." She let her gaze loose, she let it flutter and drape. "Tell me about this mystery girl." A laugh flitted by me, or a moth, then another. "There are some things you should know," she said. "We should talk."

But I knew it wasn't things I should know: it was things Momma wanted to know. She wanted to know everything I longed for. And I could tell her all of that, or I could lie. So I told her a name.

"Charmin."

"Sharon?"

"Yeah. Sharon." I watched the cartoon intensify. I scowled and reddened, hot in the cool April air. I couldn't say anything more. Her words hung unread in the air.

■

Three days later, when the daffodils bloomed and a wet snow fell, I cursed. I had never before said such words to Momma. We sat in the living room burning sappy pine logs, and Momma was in cartoon mode, filling the air with balloon words again, words about college and Sharon and graduation and the prom, and I said, "Fuck it."

She drained of color and bulged a little. She changed back; translucent white flesh crept back on her bones; her blood pulsed fast in blue knotty veins. She rounded and filled. Her words were sound now, sharp and long and hard like spears: "What did you say?" she said. "What did you say?"

A Few Casualties

So I said it again: "The prom, Momma. And Sharon. I said fuck the prom. I said fuck Sharon." Her wet mouth dangled from her chin. Cartoon mode flipped on and off like a neon sign. "Let me spell it, Momma. F-U-C-K. Fuck. Got that? Fuck the prom."

There was a long silence as she shriveled into her chair. And then, without thinking, I said, "There are other things, more important things. Like, there's the war." My voice was dry and quiet and separate from me, as though it were coming from the walls. "You know what I mean. More important things."

The next day she went to church for the first time in seven years. I started hanging out with Bernie more often, just to get away.

■

Super-Rite was the new shopping center on the state highway, across the river from our farm. It was only about a quarter-mile away, but to get there you had to drive to town, cross the Tennessee River on Evin's Bridge, and then double back north on the state highway, a total of about fifteen miles. One warm Saturday afternoon in April, three weeks before graduation, I sat with Bernie in Momma's Volkswagen in the Super-Rite parking lot, staring across the asphalt at the new grocery and the drugstore and the laundromat, lined in a row with the river flowing cold and silent behind them. Bernie's lower lip was red and swollen where his old man punched him. That's why we were here—to get away from his old man.

The Lion's Club was having its Spring Barbecue at Buckhaven Marina, which was wedged between Super-Rite and the VFW building. We could hear a brass band playing Sousa marches, bright like sunshine. Bernie lit a joint and sucked at it with his cut lip and looked at me with quick eyes paler than his skin and his hair falling dark and stringy across his eyebrows. The wind blew music through

57

the open car windows, and I reached for the joint and took a long drag, and Bernie said, "Kick ass."

I cranked the engine and we headed north on Highway 27, but after only about a hundred yards Bernie looked over his shoulder and said, "Hey Victor, pull over, man." I pulled into the huge gravel lot in front of the VFW. I looked at Bernie and said "What?" and he handed me the joint. He still looked back over his shoulder. "It's a Harley, man." He got out and walked toward a black bike parked beside a blue hand-painted plywood sign that said "VFW 225" in red letters. "Recruitment Center" was scrawled underneath it, in white. I squashed out the joint and looked nervously at some old guys in purple hats standing beside the VFW door, about fifty yards away. One of them was Bernie's uncle, Ralph Overstreet, who got his left foot blown off in Germany in 1944, but I didn't recognize the others. The old guys didn't seem to pay any attention to us, so I walked over to where Bernie squatted in the dust, running his hands across the chrome fenders of the Harley. He said, "Whose is it, you reckon?" I looked at it for a second and said, "Winkler's. Roy Winkler's." Bernie looked at me. "Ain't he dead?" I looked over my shoulder at the old men who were staring at us now, spitting into the gravel, tobacco bulging their cheeks. We could still hear the brass band at the Marina. "Come on," I said, "let's get out of here."

"Naw, man. Let's check it out." For a minute I thought he meant the Harley, but then he nodded toward a white trailer parked beside the VFW building. A sign taped to the trailer's door said "Recruitment Center Open," and Bernie turned to me and jerked his head toward it, his lower lip purple and crusted. He walked across the dusty crushed gravel and I followed him, feeling the eyes of the old men on us like pencil points jabbing, and I heard Ralph Overstreet's voice, low and indistinguishable, like boots on gravel.

A Few Casualties

A bell jingled when Bernie opened the door. I followed him into the stale black cigarette air, my lungs already heavy from the marijuana. The inside of the trailer was lined with photos of guys in uniform. Were they local folks? I didn't recognize any of them. A squirrely midget of a man in camouflage Army fatigues scrambled from behind a desk and stuck out his paw. "Gentlemen! Gentlemen!" he said. "Gentlemen!" He kept saying that over and over, as if he didn't know us. He was Bernie's cousin, Pee-Wee Overstreet, the son of Ralph Overstreet's dead brother. Pee-Wee was in the Reserves. He stood no higher than our chests.

After a while he stopped saying "Gentlemen" and just looked at us, so Bernie said, "Let's kill us some Gooks." Pee-Wee laughed and slapped him on the shoulder. "I knew," said Pee-Wee. "I knew!" He kept laughing and slapping Bernie's shoulder while "Roll Out the Barrel" played in the distance, bouncing against the sides of the trailer. Pee-Wee's nose scrunched up and his ears were crimson. He seemed to grow a few inches. Smoke came from his mouth. "Yeah! I knew you boys warn't no conscripts!" He slapped my shoulder, pawing at it, gripping it, his fingers squeezing into my skin. Then he looked me in the eye and said, "And you! You got some butt to kick, don't you, Victor? Some real personal butt to kick." He laughed again, spewing out smoke; I looked at my shoes, and he walked away.

The walls seemed to cave in a little, pressed by music and sunshine, and Bernie and Pee-Wee flattened into the wall at the other end of the trailer. They chattered like squirrels. I walked to the door and looked through a small crusted window and saw Roy Winkler, pale and light and dusty, moving without effort across crushed limestone. He seemed small and feathery: he could fly. He had gone to war and got his guts blasted loose and they tinkered with his insides, and now he could fly. I zoomed in tight on his head and saw the layered ice of his face, white, glaciated, and translucent. A bright red helmet settled over his head as the Harley wiggled between his legs. A cloud of lime dust pushed him from sight.

Pee-Wee slapped my shoulder. "Well, well," he said. "Well, well, well." He opened the door, and Bernie and I stepped out into honey-thick light. "Remember gentlemen," Pee-Wee said. "Three weeks from today. After graduation." He sneezed violently. "I'll handle the whole thing." He sneezed again. The brass band blew sunlight in and out of the air. I looked back at Pee-Wee, but he dissolved into the blackness behind him.

Bernie and I stood in the sunshine and music and shook hands. We would enlist together. We shook hands, up and down, up and down, as if we were bashing each other against the crushed gravel lot. We climbed back into the Volkswagen and sat for a while, wondering what to do next.

■

I didn't tell Momma about that visit with Pee-Wee, but she seemed to know anyway. I watched her shrink, cuddling on her sofa like a pea crawling back into its pod. She burrowed alone into her garden and her books, and suddenly her skin was dried and powdery, and she was old, the color of tired soil. Sometimes that spring I would watch from my bedroom window as she knelt in the vegetable garden, frozen in the sticky warm light. She was a photograph: her face gray and flat, her head tilted and stiff with an unnatural intensity and stillness as she stared at the honeybees dangling around the snowball bush, heavy with white flowers. She seemed posted there, like a seed packet taped to a yardstick, marking a furrow.

Bernie's promise to me and Pee-Wee meant nothing. Three days after our graduation Bernie was in Memphis living with his brother, trying to get a job on a river barge. That's what Ralph Overstreet told me one day when I found him standing alone, leaning on his cane in the shade of the covered sidewalk at Super-Rite, wearing overalls and chewing tobacco and waiting for his groceries and his wife. He talked slow and steady, the way a cow walks. I watched the whiskers jerk up and down along his jaw and watched his skin bunch up at the edges of his eyes when he looked at me. I guess he thought I would back out, the way Bernie did. I guess he kind of hoped I would.

That night, on impulse, I told Shannon I was going away to war. She laughed like falling gravel and said "Bullshit." I said, "Don't you want to see me, just once before I die," and she said, "Bullshit." I said I would probably die a perverted virgin, and she said, "Yeah, that's bullshit too." She blew hard into the receiver like rain. "I have no pity, boy. No pity at all."

I said we would meet and go on a boat ride. We would float on the current of the Tennessee River and watch the sunset. We would make a talking-machine with two empty tomato cans and some twine, and she would sit blindfolded in the bow and I would sit blindfolded in the stern and we would talk and breathe into those tomato cans. Love would be mechanical vibrations across twine. It would tweak and vibrate, pull and taunt. It would be perfect.

My laugh was dry cardboard, and I waited for her to speak. I sat sweating in the new spring heat of the upstairs room, the air stifling, thick and dark as molasses. Her breathing came like a shovel through sand. I began to pace, the floorboards moaning under my bare feet. Finally her breathing slowed and she said she wanted to see me because I was about to die. The game was over now, she said; I would die. I said "Bullshit," and she said it again, so I said, "Bullshit," and she said, "Really, I have six senses. I have a special way of knowing, and I know."

Without Bernie, I wasn't sure if I wanted to be a soldier—I didn't know what I would do. But she kept saying, "You are going to die."

So we made an agreement: we would meet, and it would be the end. I would bring a boat to the dock at Buckhaven Marina at noon the next day, and she would be waiting for me there. It would be the first time, and it would be the last time—it was that perfect.

■

I went to the Winkler place the next morning, hoping to borrow the boat from Roy, knowing the whole thing was crazy. When I got there, Roy was twenty feet up a pecan tree in what was left of Winkler's grove, among the budding branches. I could see starlings drift on currents of warm air in the gray sky above him. He was thinning out deadwood with a handsaw. I could see his muscles quivering across his shoulder bones and shivering beneath his skin, pale and solid like scorched hog skin, with bits of bark and sawdust stuck to his sweat. There were a couple of cut branches on the ground already, and the dust of the wood had spread white and even across the pale grass. Roy was muttering something to himself, something I couldn't understand. I strained to hear him, but all I heard was his saw, rhythmic, steady, and stiff, drifting like music above his mutterings, half anger, half sweat. Sweat dripped from him into the speckled dry grass, and then there was thunder.

Roy Winkler turned, high in the pecan tree, toward the thunderheads coming in from the river, and then, for the first time, I saw his scar—smooth and long and solid, running snow-white through dark hair between his nipples and arcing to his ribs. Seeing the scar like that made me shiver, as if I'd found a seashell on a mountainside or stumbled across some secret, something tucked in a family Bible or hidden under a bed. I felt like an intruder, so I turned away.

A Few Casualties

I walked to the barbed-wire fence that bordered the pasture. Suey was nibbling at clover just beyond the fence. I thought of Mary Liz on the dock, her naked body slim and pink and perfect, and then, for the first time, I wondered why Roy let her go—why he chose war and left love behind. How could he make a choice like that? Suey came toward me, blowing air through her nostrils in big dry puffs. I could hear the saw behind me, a steady rhythm going on like I wasn't there; Suey's long plodding gait thumped against the earth. She stuck her head over the fence and nudged into me gently, moving her head down toward the grass and up again, showing her teeth. I could smell her, sweet and dank and sharper than cut wood in the air. She pawed the ground and shifted her tan hooves as a quick stab of wind blew across the field, heavy with the smell of rain. Suey bobbed her head a few more times, snorting. She trotted a few feet away and looked back at me. I didn't have anything for her. She trotted into the center of the field, into some weeds.

There was another low rumble of thunder, still far away. The sawing sound stopped and I turned and saw Roy again, shiny and white, and there was that big scar across him like a lightning trail across a tree trunk. He was looking off toward the river and suddenly he looked down at me and said, "Why ain't you in school?" I said, "School's out for the summer," and he said, "Uh-huh," and spit on the tree trunk. He turned back to his work, and right away the limb he was sawing fell, hanging on a lower limb for a second before hitting the earth. He leaned back against the dark trunk and looked down at me with his saw held across his chest. "What grade you in now?" he said, and I said, "Grade?" I looked off at Suey and said, "Hell, I graduated last week. I'm eighteen." He said, "Uh-huh," and hugged the trunk as he stepped to a limb on the other side of the tree. He started sawing again.

"Old enough to get your ass shot off then, ain't you?" The sun came out and I could see the sawdust rain down, gold in the light with black chunks of bark falling, and then the sun went back in.

I looked over at Suey, still standing in the overgrown pasture. Her back was badly bowed in the middle, as though she still carried some invisible burden from her past. I knew it was from age, though; even if you never ride them, they'll get like that. She was just an old horse, nothing more.

And right then I knew that I didn't belong here anymore. I started dragging the cut limbs over to an open, weedy space where I stacked them on a big pecan stump. I walked back to Roy's tree and stood in the shower of sawdust and my mind was empty. Then I heard myself say, "I'm signing up." I swallowed hard and cleared my throat and said it a little louder. "Signing up. I'm gonna sign up."

My voice was dry and small. It was as if I didn't mean to say it, but something tight in my throat just kicked it out into the open, and there was nothing I could do about it. Roy's saw stopped. I heard him laugh—one sharp laugh—and then I heard him say, "And you got a girlfriend."

It wasn't a question, it was a statement of fact, and suddenly I realized that, just for a moment, I had forgotten why I was standing there talking to Roy Winkler in the first place. It was as if, for just a little while, Shannon didn't exist at all—as if Roy himself had to remind me of why I was here, and him not even knowing. I put the last limb on the pile and walked back to the tree and said, "Well, can I borrow the johnboat a while?" Some birds were carrying on crazy in the pecan trees as the saw hacked steadily at deadwood. I waited with sawdust floating around me and the wind picking up, and finally Roy stopped a second and looked down at me and said, "What the hell for?" I looked down at a dung beetle, dead on its back, and said, "Nothing." He looked quick at the sky and then went back to his sawing, and after a while he said, "Nothing?" Then he laughed and said, "Nothing. And even a damn lightning storm won't keep you from it." I just stood there looking up at him and finally he said, "Hell, take it, it still runs." So I walked down the path toward the river, leaving him there with his saw and his pecan grove, while thunder rolled like logs all around.

I rode the boat across the gray water of Winkler's cove and into the choppy purple flow of the main channel. Soon I could see the marina across the river. A wooden bench sat at the end of the marina's dock, and behind it was a red metal pole with a blue light on top. A pay telephone was on the pole, beneath a transparent plastic bubble. Boats lined the dock between there and the shore, tugging at their moorings. The storm was still distant and shifting, as if it revolved, trapped in a circular pattern. Wind pushed against the current, making the river appear to flow backward. I cut off the engine, wondering which way the boat would move if I let it drift.

I stretched out in the bottom of the boat, watching the clouds move across the sky and listening to thunder roll across the Cumberland Plateau. After a while darker clouds moved in, lower in the sky, and the boat began to slowly spin. Spits of lightning spewed inside the clouds, and river water hit the sides of the metal boat like tiny drumming fingers. I felt thunder dulling deep in the river below me as lightning tickled the air, charging it against my skin. After a while I sat up. The storm was all around me but no rain fell, and it seemed the boat hadn't drifted at all, though the wind had scrambled the surface of the water to a frantic chop.

I looked toward the marina. Shannon still wasn't there.

What if she had been? What would I have done? I mindlessly cranked the engine and guided the boat toward the marina. Then I pushed the rudder hard to the right and turned the boat back toward the opposite shore, toward Winkler's cove. I felt suddenly anxious; could it be that someone was standing there on Winkler's rotted dock, waving to me, beckoning me to return? I scanned the shoreline, half expecting (against my better judgment) to see something or someone waiting for me there. But there was nothing to see, only the mouth of the cove and the tangles of willows and oaks along the shore. The dock itself was not even visible from the main channel—I knew that. But for some reason I again cut the engine, letting the boat drift as I looked into the trees, watching them sway back and forth in the wind. What was I looking for? Or, should I say, who was I looking for? Was it Roy? I knew better, of course; it was only when I closed my eyes that I could see him, sitting stiffly on Winkler's dock in a single beam of sunshine, frozen as though trapped in amber, with his purple striped trunks and his sunglasses and his orange beach towel, his body whole again, his eyes fixed on something in the distance, somewhere across the water. Mary Liz Barter lay on her back beside him, the transistor radio inches from her head, her eyes closed, her naked body red and stiff like wax, shiny in the light. And in that same light I saw Momma on her knees in the black earth of a garden, rooted and motionless like a sprout. Behind her, Suey stood frozen in profile, and in the saddle sat a soldier, erect, smooth as polished marble. His uniform was spotless and perfect but strangely indistinct—featureless and anonymous like his face. And I asked myself: is this the sort of thing it all reduces to? These vignettes? Little sculptures in the mind? I opened my eyes to bolts of lightning scattering through the treetops around Winkler's cove, and I thought of the real Roy, the scarred one I had left in the pecan grove, trimming deadwood. If he could see all this, what would he say? What advice could he give me?

Lightning still came in quick branchings above the trees as I cranked the engine, turned the boat toward the empty marina, and rode to shore. I pulled the bow of the boat onto dry land beside the marina's main dock and tied it to a tree root with a piece of nylon cord. I walked to the dock and stood there alone for a while, watching the boats tug at their moorings in the wind.

Finally the phone at the end of the dock began to ring. The rushing air smelled like rain and the clouds pressed low and the thunder seemed closer, and that phone rang and rang. After a while I turned from it and walked across a weedy field toward the VFW on Highway 27, and even from there I could hear that phone ringing behind me. It rang for a long, long time. The dust on the gravel lot rose in silent eddies and crossed the highway into the trees, and the rain never came.

Goats
The Courtship of Dixie Pepper

I.

When I was in the Army I had a dog named Muck. He was a good dog, the kind of dog that just walks up and gets friendly and he's your pal for life. He had eyes that seemed like they could talk—a sign of a really good dog—and he lived with me and my high school buddy Karlen O'Malley and a bunch of other guys in a quonset hut on a hunk of coral called Eniwetok, in the South Pacific, a place where the Army exploded nuclear bombs to prove they could make bigger bangs than the Russians could. Every other day for about two months we exploded a plain "battlefield" A-bomb, and every now and then we did one of the big hydrogen ones, too, the compact kind designed to go on those missiles the Army planned to blow up the world with. My job was to help another fellow do part of the final "arming" of the A-bombs after the Air Force flew them in from the lab, so naturally we felt like we were the big cheese that made it happen, even though it was really about as complicated as setting an alarm clock, no big deal—a trained monkey could've done it. And it wasn't long before Muck the dog became Muck the blind dog because, being a dog, he didn't have enough sense to cover his eyes when the bombs went off. The X-rays from those bombs burned his eyeballs out. There came a time when old Muck would walk into trees and walls, and he was the laughingstock of the whole garrison. He was sick, too. His hair fell out, he had big sores on his skin, he spit up blood. He was pitiful, and those blank eyes just stared right through me, saying, "This is what *you* did, so what the hell you gonna do about it?" All I could do was feel bad and scratch his belly a lot, and sometimes Karlen managed to get him steak from the mess sergeant. Then one day me and a couple of lab guys were at the airfield rolling a bomb trigger across the tarmac in a little red wagon when old Muck wandered up under the wing of a B-52 and laid down and died. I put Muck in the wagon with the triggering device of a ten-megaton hydrogen bomb and took him with us across the lagoon to the blast site. I laid him underneath the tower where they installed the bomb, and when it blew, Muck was vaporized instantly. When they let us look at it, I saw every color of the rainbow in that fireball. It was an especially big blast. The shock wave knocked everybody flat on their asses in the sand, even though we were five miles away. I laid there in that sand thinking about how Muck's atoms were up inside that mushroom cloud, and it seemed like he was all around when the ash settled on everything. Old Muck was fallout. I'll never forget Muck.

I suppose I should've learned something about responsibility from Muck—how responsibility is as much a part of life as air or water or dirt, whether we admit it or not—but Eniwetok was a long time ago, and I was just a kid. It was many years later, after I got into an embarrassing mess involving Dixie Pepper, Oscar McNairy, my wife, and a goat, that Muck's lesson finally started to slowly sink in.

■

Old Oscar McNairy always said that when things change, people should change too, and that's how you get to know what people are really like. That was true of Dixie Pepper, I guess. A few months after her daddy died, Dixie Pepper walked into Tangerine's Bucktooth Bakery (where she had been working since she moved back home from New York, two years earlier) and talked Tangerine into a special deal so she wouldn't have to do any batter-mixing or cake-baking or pan-scubbing anymore—she would just show up in the afternoons and spread the frosting on.

That bothered lots of people around here. It just didn't seem right. "Who does she think she is?" Tangerine said real loud so everybody could hear. Me and Oscar McNairy were sitting at the counter at Tangerine's, drinking coffee. "She acts like she's some kind of goddess or something."

I stuck my nose down close to my coffee cup and sniffed. "Don't know about that," I said. "Don't know what to think about Dixie Pepper."

Tangerine just grunted. She cleared some dirty dishes off the counter and banged them down hard in the sink.

"A goddess she ain't," said Oscar, "but she sure looks like one."

I looked at his smiling eyes and he winked and I gave him a look that said, "Watch it, old man."

"Get you a goddess while the gettin's good," said Oscar. He elbowed me in the forearm and laughed, then sipped some coffee. "Got a good shot at her this time, Hal."

Tangerine frowned at us. "Dixie ain't no goddess," she said, rubbing the counter with a rag that smelled like a pine tree would smell if you poked one up your nose. "She's rich, and that ain't the same as being a goddess."

"That's right," I said. "Lots of rich people ain't goddesses, not even close." I looked at Oscar.

"Well, maybe that's true," said Oscar. "I don't know." He shrugged and took another sip of coffee. "Your average goddess," he said, "has got to be at least middle class, don't you reckon, Hal?"

I nodded and said, "Yeah, Oscar, that's about right," and Tangerine just shook her head and stepped back into the kitchen.

■

Of course, it soon became common knowledge that Dixie Pepper was the richest unmarried woman around. The first thing she did, about three weeks after her daddy Red was officially dead and gone, was to have the backyard dug up and a blue concrete swimming pool put in, right where the poinsettias used to be. And it wasn't long before Dixie sold three-hundred-fifty acres of Red's best farmland to the Chatt-Ham Development Company out of Chattanooga, the company run by Ham Buckley, who used to be mayor of Chattanooga until he decided that bringing in a million dollars a year would be even better. Ham built the indoor mall and a two-hundred-fifty lot subdivision in eight months flat, figuring Bucktooth Haven was close enough to Chattanooga to bring out the yuppies and old folks—and if not, well, it was no hair off his hide. He'd come out with a million one way or the other, the way millionaires always do.

Dixie's daddy was rumored to have quite a stash put away. Dixie's momma, Lora Lee, had been dead for over forty years—she got run over by a runaway potato chip truck during a snowstorm in downtown Chattanooga, right after Dixie was born. So the Pepper fortune was Dixie's, flat out, no strings attached. In short, Dixie Pepper was independently wealthy—an unusual thing for a single, good-looking woman in Bucktooth Haven, Tennessee.

Even though she was about forty-something years old when her daddy died, she didn't look a day over thirty. And I guess you could say that after Red's funeral there wasn't a guy within fifty miles of Bucktooth Haven who, somewhere deep inside his private self, didn't want a piece of Dixie Pepper.

■

Of course, years before, I'd had my chance at Dixie Pepper and I was too much a fool to follow through. I was barely eighteen—a deep well of ignorance, that's what an eighteen-year-old boy is. It's the kind of ignorance that's like a chalkboard sitting there waiting for somebody to come along and write on it. And if the person holding the chalk is ignorant, too, then you got ignorance on top of ignorance, which is the way the world works, I guess.

It was mostly Oscar who held the chalk in those days, filling in the blanks of my younger life with baseball and football and chores and those damn fool schemes of his. One day he came by the house and says, "Let's go over to the Pepper place," and I said, "What for?" and he says, "To help Red Pepper with them pine trees that fell across the bob-wire fence," and I said, "Which bob-wire fence?" and he says, "The one down by the river," and I said, "I didn't know they had a bob-wire fence down by the river," and he says, "They's a lot of things you don't know, boy." And he said that in a way that made me feel like a idiot just because I didn't know that Red Pepper had a fence in that overgrown tangle of useless bottomland.

So we got in Oscar's truck, which in those days was a one-ton flat-

73

bed GMC, and drove down the river road toward the Pepper place, and as we drove along Oscar starts talking about "that heifer." "Red needs help with that heifer," he'd say, gunning that old truck over chuckholes and grinning at me like I was up to some kind of mischief that I didn't even know I was up to. So I'd just look out at the river or across to the mountains without saying anything. And after a while Oscar would say something like, "Yep, that's some heifer." Oscar had to yell to make me hear him over the sound of the truck's engine, which didn't have a muffler. I just kept quiet, looking out at the river, which was in a flood stage from heavy rains. The truck bounced over the ruts in that muddy road like some kind of circus ride. "Yep, Hal," says Oscar, "you don't see many heifers like that one around here."

Finally he stopped the truck at a place where the river had come up over the road, so I turned to him and said, "Hell, Oscar, Red Pepper ain't had any cattle since he went into the hardware business, you know that."

Oscar looked at the flooded road and then at me and says, "It ain't cattle we're talking about, boy." He seemed kind of worried when he said it, but then he grinned and poked me in the ribs in a way that made me see all of a sudden what he was saying. I just said "Shee-it" and probably turned red or something, so I looked out at the river churning by us while Oscar gunned the engine as hard as he could and we both bounced up to the roof as that old truck jumped across the ruts and cut through that bit of river water laying across the road. We drove the rest of the way to the Pepper place without saying anything.

We pulled in next to the barn and Oscar says, "There's Dixie over there beside them apple trees, Hal." He slapped me on the shoulder and says, "Go on over and see her. Go on, Hal."

It was early spring and I could smell the apple blossoms in the air. Even though I was a young man, and even though I liked girls the way young men are supposed to, for some reason I didn't want to even look in the direction of them apple trees. I'd known Dixie for years—we went to Bucktooth Haven Baptist Church together and to Bucktooth Haven School together—but she had always been in the background, just a skinny girl too young for me to worry with, shy and quiet, the kind of limp little fragile thing that just gets buffeted along like a little piece of cork in a river and would never amount to much in life, it seemed to me. I was a high school senior then, about to graduate in a few weeks, and I had my eye on other girls, the ones my age that looked more like what I figured women were supposed to look like. So I just ignored Oscar and walked across the mud into the barn, where Red Pepper was sharpening his axe.

Red Pepper was a big man with a red face and red hair and a hard look about him. I remembered him mostly from church, the way he'd sit all alone on the pew, hunched like a bear with his Bible close to his face and his lips kind of moving and his finger tracing along the page as he read. I don't think I'd ever seen him smile or frown or anything. He was a mountain, solid and quiet—that's the best way to describe him. But that day, when I walked into the barn, he got up from the grindstone and looked me in the eyes and held out his hand, and his lips moved back in a kind of smile almost. I didn't know what to do—it was the first time in my life Red Pepper had ever acknowledged my existence.

"Hal," he says. So I shook his hand. Then we both looked at Oscar, who seemed to be watching awful close.

"Well," says Red finally, looking away. "Time to go, I reckon."

We walked across his good pasture, ducked under a barbed-wire fence, and stepped into the trees near the river. Sure enough, there was another old fencerow back in there, with a single pine tree lying across it. We did the work without saying a word, which is not so unusual for Red but was mighty unusual for Oscar McNairy. We had that tree cut and the fence restrung in about twenty minutes, and the whole time I wondered why Red needed us just for this.

And then, while we were just standing there for a minute looking at the fence kind of absently, the way you always do when a job is done, Red leans his axe against a tree trunk and says, "The thing is, you can work with me. That is, if you want to." He coughed into his fist. "I'll set you up at the hardware store."

At first I didn't know he was talking to me. He was looking up into the trees when he said it. But Oscar poked me on the arm, so I said, "Huh?" and Red cleared his throat and said it again.

Then Red looks at me and squirms a little and says, "You know, boy—your daddy. I, uh—" and he coughed again and cleared his throat, reaching for his axe. He gave Oscar a hard stare, looked back at me, and said, "What I mean is—well, your daddy. And Iwo Jima. Iwo Jima and all that." And he looked back at Oscar again, and then started walking back toward the house without us.

I looked at Oscar and he looks kind of sheepish and says, "What Red is trying to say, Hal, is that, well—you're about to graduate and all that, so we figure you're gonna need some help."

I shrugged. I hadn't really thought about it much.

"So the plan," says Oscar, "is for you to work with Red, as a partner. He's offering you a damn good career, Hal." Oscar looked down at the ground for a minute, and still I didn't say anything. Then he said, "And there's more to it than that, too." He cleared his throat. "You see, ol' Red Pepper, he's kind of old-fashioned, and well, the fact of the matter is, Hal—Red wants you to get married."

"What?"

"Red wants you to get married."

I just looked at Oscar.

"Married?"

"Yeah."

"Well, who the hell to? I can't just waltz out and get married!"

"He wants you to marry Dixie Pepper."

"Dixie?" I kind of laughed and stared at Oscar some more. "What the hell you mean, Oscar?"

"Now I know what you're thinking, Hal," says Oscar. "But this is not as uncommon a thing as you might think. It's one of them arranged kinds of things. You know. See, Red's from the old school when it comes to things like this. He was one of your daddy's close friends, you know, like me. Old soldiers, Iwo Jima, all that, and he keeps his commitments and all. I mean—"

"So he wants me to marry Dixie Pepper?"

"Yeah, that's about the size of it."

"And what about Dixie?"

"Well, what about her?" he said. He looked at me like I was some kind of fool.

"Well, how does she feel about all this?"

"Feel?" Oscar shrugged. "Hell, she's sixteen, Hal."

We stood quiet for a minute just listening to the breeze in the trees. Then we started back toward the house, and Oscar said, "Just think about it, that's all. You ain't got to do anything you don't want to do."

The walk back to the truck was the longest, scariest, and most wonderful walk of my life. I felt like I was no longer attached to the same planet I'd spent all my life on. Oscar, Red, the truck, the farm, the river—it all seemed changed somehow, as though it had suddenly transformed into some kind of enormous circus ride—an artificial world built to amuse me, like one of them floats they have in the Strawberry Festival parade in downtown Chattanooga.

As we passed the barn I looked off toward the orchard. Dixie was still there, and I stopped dead in my tracks, staring at her. It seemed like Dixie, too, had changed into something else—some kind of creature I'd never seen before—during the few minutes we had been out working on that fence.

I saw her in a beam of sunlight beneath one of the blossoming apple trees, her back to me, about fifty feet away. She was working on a painting. She had it propped up on one of those artist's easels, but I couldn't tell what the picture was, and I didn't really care. All I could see was her hair, red and long and shiny—the way it floated across her shoulders and down past the small of her back like some kind of silky fabric. She had on a long, flowery dress that reached almost to the ground, and the sunlight was just right so that, when she shifted her weight, I could see the outline of her hips and legs as they moved gently beneath her skirt. I just stood and gaped at her. She was beautiful. And, according to the world Red and Oscar had set up for me, she was mine for the taking.

■

So I go into a kind of trance for a few weeks, unable to be myself anymore, the way boys always get when they're all worked up over a girl. Finally Oscar convinces me to ask her to the Senior Dance, so I show up at the Pepper place one afternoon in Oscar's GMC flatbed truck. I was a little relieved when nobody came to the door, but as I was about to leave I noticed somebody in the barn, back in the shadows of it. I figured it might be Red in there, so I stepped inside, and there was Dixie, just standing, for no apparent reason, in the runway between the stables. Her eyes were big and round, looking right at me, and a smile came up on her face as I stood staring at her.

"Hi," she said.

"Hi," I said right back.

I saw her eyes scan down to my feet and back up to my head and back down again, and she put her hand over her mouth and kind of giggled. It was then that I saw her daddy. I could see him through the open door at the other end of the barn, behind her. He was walking away real fast, across the pasture toward the river. I saw him stop, look back toward the barn, and then continue on.

"So," I said.

She just smiled at me.

"So you helping your daddy?" I said.

She kept smiling and said, "Do what?"

"Oh, I don't know. Working in the barn here, I reckon. Whatever."

She giggled.

"Well," I said. There was a long pause. "Well, then. I reckon you'll come with me to the Senior Dance, huh?"

She giggled again and then looked serious and then giggled some more. And then she laughed. It was the damnedest thing, something I wouldn't have guessed in a million years, the way she laughed like that, because she wasn't just giggling anymore, the way shy girls do. This was big, straight-from-the-gut laughing, the way you laugh at something that is completely crazy. I just stood there staring and she tried to stop, putting one hand on my shoulder and the other across her mouth with her eyes twinkling real bright at me and her cheeks flushed, but her face scrunched up again with laughter until it got to the point where, the harder she tried not to, the harder she laughed. To her credit, she did calm down long enough to talk a little bit, but it wasn't much. She just said, "Like a sack of potatoes," and she laughed some more and got her breath and said, "And you fall for it! You think you can just come in here like this and walk away with a sack of potatoes!" And again she went into such hysterics that I just walked away.

I did look back over my shoulder, though, just one time, and at that very instant she stopped laughing and gave an almost pained expression. For just that instant she looked genuinely concerned about something and she waved her arm, beckoning me to come back. That was my chance, my only real chance at Dixie Pepper, and if I'd taken it I'd be a rich man today. Instead I just got in the truck and left her there, alone in that barnyard.

I didn't go to the dance. I did join the Army, though, two days after graduation. I didn't tell Oscar or anybody else until the day I left for boot camp. And I found out later that Dixie Pepper had moved to New York at about the same time I'd joined the Army. She moved in with some of her momma's relatives who lived up there. She finished her schooling and lived there for years. She even went to some kind of art school in New York City.

Of course there were those rumors about her having a stillborn baby right after moving up there. I never found out any of the details of that, though, and I don't want to know, either. Some things are better left a mystery.

As for me, I took an honorable discharge from the Army three years later. Then I married Ellie Fowler, a girl I'd known since I was a little boy.

Ellie was tall, big-boned, functional, the kind of woman a man needs if he's going to build himself a life in this world. I won her hand fair and square, the way you're supposed to do—with dates and candy and nice dinners in town. She liked how I looked in my uniform, and I had a good job lined up, too, doing high explosives over at the marble quarry, a skill I'd learned in the Army.

And the fact is, Ellie really loved me. She said so herself. She said, "Dammit, *yes,* Hal. Of course I love you. Why the hell do you think I'd go out with you all the goddamn time if I didn't love you?"

Anyway, I had had my chance at Dixie Pepper—a chance that a

lot of guys around here would kill for. And when Dixie moved back home, years later, I didn't think much of it. In spite of what folks around here say, me and Dixie didn't have much to do with each other after she moved back—at least, not until that goat got loose.

II.

One hot day in late August, two years after Red Pepper died, I was sitting in my Dodge Dart station wagon in a shady spot beside the kerosene pump at Chuckie's store, waiting for the doughnut man. Three days earlier my wife Ellie had kicked me out of the house for the third time in as many months, and I was living in a little hole of a room above Chuckie's store. But I still held out hope that I could get back into her good graces, so I was sitting there waiting on the Krispy Kreme man to bring me forty-two dozen doughnuts for the Third Annual Orphans' Drive, sponsored by Cub Scout Den 44—of which Ellie was chief den mother. After a while Oscar drove up in his new four-by-four monster truck and parked next to me. He was drinking from a can of Budweiser, and right away I noticed he had a big, ugly black eye. He leaned his self against my car, poked his head into my open window, and said that a couple of hours earlier he got assaulted, victimized, and abused by Hank, the runaway billy goat.

"Now hold on," I said to Oscar. "Hank ain't my billy goat no more. Everybody knows that."

Oscar took a swig of the Budweiser and looked up at the sky. "Oh," he said. "I reckon I didn't hear about that." He ran a finger across his black eye and started telling how not only did Hank the goat kick his face in, but, even worse, he ate Dixie Pepper's brand-new exercise tape and part of her poor dead daddy's stamp collection, and a quilt, and is still running loose. I spit into a empty Styrofoam

81

coffee cup and looked at the swollen red spot on the bridge of Oscar's nose and said, "Well, now," and he says, "Yep," and I said, "Now if that don't beat all," and he says, "Uh-huh."

I ran my hands across the steering wheel.

"Goats," I said. "They get loose."

"Yep," says Oscar. "That's goats."

He took a big swig of the Budweiser and burped. Then he lit a Lucky Strike and we were quiet for a while, just enjoying the shade, and finally I said, "Well, what was you doing out at the Pepper place, anyway?" and he kind of frowns and looks off across the parking lot at nothing in particular. After a minute he says, "Why, I was out there chasing that fool goat, what the hell you think I was doing?"

I knew right then that he was lying, but it's always been my nature to go along with somebody when I know they're lying, especially Oscar, since he'd always been like a daddy to me. So I just looked him right in the eyes and waited for him to continue his story, and he bent down close to me again. His whiskers were little black pins stuck in his cheeks, which sunk in like a melon with a bad spot, and I could smell his breath like sour milk and tuna fish, even though he had a lit Lucky in one hand and a can of Bud in the other.

"It's like this, Hal," Oscar says. "I was just driving along the River Road on my way to town to get some motor oil and was passing by the Pepper place, you know, and I looked up and seen that goat crash through the middle of a big picture window. Landed in a firethorn bush." He straightened up, stepped back, and leaned against his four-by-four, crossing his arms. The cigarette hung from his lips and sent smoke streaming in front of his face. "And you know what I said? I says to myself, I said, That there goat is *loose!*"

"Hold on now," I said to Oscar. "You mean it was inside the house?"

"Hell yeah," he says to me, dropping his cigarette on the ground. "It was *in,* and jumped *out.* I seen it. Right through the picture window. It seen me coming and lit out across the backyard, heading for those beehives that Red bought off them hippies."

Oscar spit into the dust and stood up straight and doused the cigarette butt with the rest of his Budweiser. His belly hung out over his jeans, and I noticed something that looked like spaghetti sauce splattered on his shirt.

"Hell, Oscar, what'd you do?" I said.

"Well, there wasn't much I could do. I went up on the porch to the picture window and seen all the broken glass, and looked in and seen all the mess it made inside, and I hollered in, 'Dixie Pepper, you OK?' over and over, but she didn't answer, so I crawled in through the busted window and hollered 'Dixie Pepper, you in there? Dixie Pepper, you in there?' Lord, let me tell you, she was fit to be tied when she found out about them Buns of Steel."

"How it eat a tape like that?" I said to Oscar.

"Just ate the tape part," he says back. "Pulled it out like spaghetti and left the shell. Ate a Dr. Ruth tape, too." He shook his head and started cleaning his fingernails with his Barlow pocketknife. "Hell, them blame tapes cost forty, fifty bucks. And the thing to play it with? Lord God Almighty!"

"Yeah," I said. I spit into the cup again. "A rich man's game."

"You got that right," he says.

We were quiet for a long time, listening to some cicadas in the trees, until finally I said, "Well anyway, Oscar, what you think Hank the goat was doing all the way over at the Pepper place, anyhow?" Oscar stood up straight and looked across the parking lot toward Chuckie's store. A slight breeze picked up, and some leaves fell from the big tree above my car.

"Why, I was hoping you could tell *me* that, Hal. I thought she borrowed him from you."

"*Borrowed* him? From me?"

"Everybody knows it was your billy goat."

"Hell, Oscar, everybody but you knows I sold it to A.C. Hixson's boy Rollo, like I done told you."

"Why'd you want to go sell your billy goat for?"

"What business is it of yours?"

"Just wondering, Hal, that's all."

There was another long silence and finally I said, "Hell Oscar, I sold Hank, all of my rabbits, and Ellie's Japanese three-wheeler to Rollo Hixson. I needed some lawyer money."

Oscar, he looks up sharp at me, and even though one of his eyes was goat-kicked, he still stares straight through me, like he always has whenever I made any kind of decision on my own. All my life it's been that way. He looked at me like that when I joined the Army, and then when I married Ellie, and then when I started neglecting Ellie, and then when I started trying to fix things with Ellie—and countless other times, ever since I was just a boy. He was like Muck, my old Army dog—his eyes could talk. And I guess the one thing that is always there between me and Oscar is his disapproval of my marrying Ellie. When the preacher said, "Does anyone here object to this marriage," Oscar starts waving his arms and jumping around, yelling, "I do, I do," and Alvin Fowler, Ellie's daddy, had to go grab him by the collar and make him shut up by threatening to pull his teeth out one by one. And now that he thinks I'm finally trying to divorce her, Oscar looks at me that way again, like I'm some kind of damn fool.

"So you're going through with it," he says. He says it in a whisper, almost.

"Look, Oscar," I say. "I got a lawyer, but not because I want out of the marriage. It's because I want to know what my options are. I just don't know what to do, Oscar."

He stares at me like I'm crazy, his mouth hanging open and his eyebrows raised up. "Shee-it," he says finally. "Don't know what to do, my ass." He took a long look at the empty Budweiser can, then looked up at the sky, and right then the Krispy Kreme doughnut truck pulled up and the driver got out, so Oscar didn't say what it was he was about to say. Instead he said, "Well, what we gonna do about that goat?"

I shrugged. "Tell Rollo Hixson, I guess."

"I guess." Oscar turned, as if he was about to leave.

"But Oscar," I said, "there's just one thing I don't quite get."

"About what?"

"About this goat business." I spit into the coffee cup again. "Tell me this—why in the world would anybody want to *borrow* a billy goat?"

There was a long pause and Oscar narrowed his eyes and leaned in close to me. "Maybe it's for them pictures she draws," he said. "She don't do nothing but draw pictures all day, you know." He lowered his voice. "But it seems like somehow it's more than that." He looked back over his shoulder and then leaned down even closer to me. "Let me tell you something. I got this feeling about her—I think that gal's *up* to something. And it ain't exactly natural neither." He spit into the dust. "Don't go getting any more mixed up with her than you already are, Hal. Times has changed. As a friend, I'm telling you—"

"Now Oscar—"

He raised his hand. "It don't matter, save it. Just remember what I told you, that's all." Oscar was grinning, in a grim kind of way. He walked across the parking lot, crushed the Budweiser can, threw it in the cardboard trash box next to the kerosene pump, and yanked open

Chuckie's screen door. As it swung shut behind him I saw him look back at me and wink that swollen black eye, with that grin still on his face like it was painted there, and I knew right then he was up to something—something that probably had to do with me and Dixie Pepper and all those rumors that had been going around about us lately. But I knew I'd find out little else from Oscar McNairy.

■

Here's what you should know about Oscar—how he's always messing around in other people's business and then lying about it. Whatever he says is most likely at least part lie, but there's always enough truth in it to make you wonder what the hell really happened. The thing is, Oscar *knows* you know he's lying, and not only that—he knows you also know there's a smidgen of truth somewhere in there but you can't tell exactly what it is. When I was a boy, sometimes I'd go down to the breakfast table and there would be Oscar, sitting in my kitchen having coffee and pancakes with my momma. Oscar used to be a little weasly guy with skinny shoulders and a bird beak nose, but in his later years he got a round belly that made him look pregnant. For the life of me I never understood why some women liked him, but apparently they did—Chuckie says Oscar had affairs with just about every woman in Bucktooth Haven in his day, even with Ellie's mother, Sarah Fowler. On those mornings Oscar would walk me out to the school bus, telling me some story about him and Red Pepper and my daddy, about how they always used to be involved in some kind of craziness around Bucktooth Haven before they went off to war together. I always believed him, every word— until I got old enough to realize I wasn't really supposed to. Like, there was that story about how one time, late one Saturday night, Oscar got a crosscut saw and him and my daddy and Red sawed the steeple off of Bucktooth Haven Baptist Church, which is the Salvation Army store now. Oscar claims they got a winch and tackle and lifted Preacher Parkinson's cow Millie up on top of the church and tied her at the spot where the steeple used to be, and later they sat and watched from the feed store across the road while the congregation stood looking up at that cow and that cow stood looking down at the congregation, chewing its cud and bellowing like it was about to explode. And Oscar says that finally Preacher Parkinson, who was late because he had been out since dawn looking for his cow Millie, came barreling up in his Dusenberg and got down on his knees in the parking lot and went into holy-rolling spasm fits, yelling, "Praise the Lord, praise His Holy Name! My precious Millie's come home at last!"

Now that part is crazy enough, and that's not even all of it. Since it was hours past milking time, says Oscar, Preacher Parkinson got a ladder from the church shed and a fill-bucket from the baptistry and climbed up to where the steeple used to be and milked that cow right then and there while his wife, Miss Liza, the song leader, got everybody to start singing "Bound for the Promised Land," right there in the parking lot. Now that's just a sample of the kind of thing Oscar claimed was true, without expecting you to believe all of it, maybe not even much of it. But what bugs me is that, even though it seems like I might've read a story a lot like that one in a book somewhere, and even though every time Oscar tells me the story some little detail about it changes, and even though I can tell something's up by the way his eyes kind of shine and dance and the way his voice rises like a question mark when he tells it, the fact is some of the people around town—like Barney Milton at the barbershop—claim that, yes indeed, it happened, or *something* like that happened. After all, says Barney Milton, there ain't a steeple on the Salvation Army store anymore is there? And besides, he says, everybody knows what a prankster Oscar McNairy was and always has been and always will be, until his dying day.

One story I've always wanted to hear from Oscar is the story of how my father died, and for some reason he could never bring himself to tell it. All I know is what my mother's brother from Georgia, Uncle Al, told me one time at Thanksgiving Dinner: that his legs were blown off by some kind of mine or bomb on a beach in the South Pacific, and that Oscar was there when it happened. Red Pepper was there, too. And it could be that it was too painful for Oscar to recall, or he thought it was maybe too gruesome for me to ever know. But sometimes I think he never told me because it was really pretty straightforward, because there was no foolery about it, and no real drama about it, no details you could play around with to make it sound better than real life—it simply was what it was and nothing more, and there was nothing he could say or do that would make it into a story more worth telling than what I already knew.

■

Well, the fact is I had been in a mess with Ellie for the better part of a year now, and no matter how much I tried to make it sound like it was her fault, the truth is I was probably the one to blame. Part of it was because I got laid off from the quarry. They laid us all off and shut the place down. Then I spent all spring and summer down at Darnell's Dive Den, drinking with old Army buddies like Karlen O'Malley and Newt Hixson, or with younger guys like Chuckie or his cousin Marty the lawyer, letting them macho-bull me into saying and doing things I didn't really mean to say and do.

Chuckie and Marty the lawyer had never had wives of their own; they were ex-football jocks in their early thirties, and they would show up after work and we'd stand at the bar and scratch our balls and spit on the floor and watch baseball on TV, chugging Coors and talking about money problems, or car problems, or leaky roof problems, or plumbing problems, or woman problems, anything that seemed like a problem. It was a ritual, a kind of communion. I'd complain about something and they'd agree, and for some reason that felt awfully good to me. I might say something like, "Ellie kicked my ass last night," so Marty, he'd say, "Shee-it," and I'd say, "Okay, okay, but she may as well have," and Chuckie'd say something like, "Well screw her, Hal, just screw her," and I'd say, "Yeah, screw her." I'd say, "Where's a man's freedom? Where's a man's basic respect in life?"

And the fact is, during those nights at the Dive Den, the truth about Ellie didn't matter all that much. We'd sit on the barstools listening to George Jones on the jukebox, pretending we were just like old George—victims of whiskey and women and marriage. Marty or Chuckie might say, "Women, you can't live with 'em, can't live without 'em," and I'd say, "Yeah, women, can't live with 'em, can't live without 'em," and things would kind of spin around me and we'd say things about Ellie and women that, I'll admit, don't seem exactly fair now that I think back on it.

And it could be that somehow during those nights at the Dive Den, I started to create an Ellie in my mind that grew further and further from who Ellie really was. On those nights things would spin around me and my whole life seemed like one big, dizzy, nuclear-powered circus ride. Sometimes Marty the lawyer's head would seem to be stuck inside his neck and he would turn it around toward me like a giant turtle head and say, "I can fix it, man, anytime, you just let me know and I'll fix it. I can make you a free man." And this went on and on until it seemed like life itself, and my own lies seemed to be truer than what I knew to be true.

And I'll be damned if I didn't accept Marty's offer one day after I'd been living in the little rat-hole room above Chuckie's store for three days already because Ellie wouldn't let me in the house. I was on a drunk, that's the bare fact of the matter. So I told Marty to get started, to push those papers and make me a new life. I said—and I remember this exactly—I said, "Go ahead, Marty, make my day," and there was lots of laughing and backslapping and general good-old-boy fun at the Dive Den that night.

I was on a damn drunk, that's all it was, and later that night when I felt hollow in my belly and cold and alone in that little junky room at Chuckie's, tired of it all, Ellie let me come back home. Why, I don't know, but when I felt the warmth of her hug as I walked through the front door, and when I saw the tear on her cheek as she tried real hard to smile at me, and when I saw our eight-year-old son Hal Junior sitting there building dive bombers out of Legos beside the fireplace, I regretted a hundred times over having even *met* that damn Marty the lawyer. I folded myself back into the family again like a pea going back into its pod, and it was nice while it lasted. I even called up Marty the lawyer's office and got one of those answering machines, and I didn't even wait for the beep, I just started telling him to go jump in a canoe and paddle fast to hell, because I'm a happily married man.

■

Of course, three weeks later Ellie threw me out again, and this time it was worse than ever. Tangerine, of Tangerine's Bucktooth Bakery, being a bored person with not much excitement in her life, teamed up with Oscar McNairy (as best as I can tell) and started the rumor that I snuck up, unbidden, and pinched Dixie Pepper's wagging behind while Dixie was putting a paisley tuxedo on a G.I. Joe doll that was going on top of Heather Putter's oversized Rock 'n' Roll wedding cake. And of course it was a damn lie—if Tangerine had seen what really happened from up close instead of hiding behind the Coke machine she'd know that Dixie pinched *my* butt *first*, while I was doing nothing in the world but standing there with my empty Styrofoam coffee cup waiting on a refill. But no, Tangerine was hiding behind the Coke machine, looking for trouble. And by the time the story got into Oscar's brain and spread around town to Ellie, it had grown into a long torrid love affair, a series of liaisons at the Holiday Inn in Chattanooga, and next thing you know I'm back in the little room above Chuckie's store, spending time with Chuckie and Marty the lawyer yet again, down at the Dive Den. Life just keeps happening over and over.

But hell, at this point all I can say is, what does it really matter? Where does the truth come in? I guess there's a point where what really happens in your life just don't matter, and what people *think* happened becomes the big thing. Certainly telling Ellie the truth of what happened at Tangerine's was worse than any lies—I learned firsthand that there's no way you can hold a marriage together by arguing over who pinched whose butt first. It just don't help.

All this has a lot to do with why things turned out the way they did—in particular, why I finally did get tangled up (in a real odd way) with Dixie Pepper; why I ended up living for good in that rat-hole junkroom above Chuckie's store; and why, in the end, Oscar McNairy ended up dead.

III.

When I arrived home for the Third Annual Krispy Kreme meeting of Cub Scout Den 44, I pulled in behind Oscar's four-by-four monster truck and just sat there a while. Oscar lived about a hundred yards down the road, on the land next to mine, and because Oscar was always hanging around on Cub Scout day anyway, it was no real surprise to see him there now. There I was with a car full of dough-nuts, thinking, "Yeah, this'll patch things up; stuff like this is all it takes"—as if doughnuts were some kind of magic marriage potion; as if you can take a bomb that's exploded and glue it back together again, just like that. Looking back, I wonder if that's the kind of thinking that kept me married to Ellie for so long. When the going got rough I always figured I could stick things back together, and when things *did* stick back together somehow, I always told myself it was because of something I did, like fixing the toilet or roofing the house or helping with the dishes or finally making her pregnant. Keeping the marriage alive was like doing penance, a series of reded-ications. Why should it be any different now?

I could hear the Cub Scouts inside the house making all kinds of racket. It was a beautiful day for a change. The sky was blue like it got crayoned that way, and the clouds were like somebody had took cotton puffs out of aspirin bottles and pasted them up there, and I guess for a few minutes I did feel pretty good, watching old Bart the cat stretching out and purring in the sunshine beside the azalea bush.

I heard the screen door whang open on the porch, so I got out of the car. Ellie came marching across the yard in her den mother's uni-form, which was really a den daddy's uniform because that was all the Salvation Army had, and besides, she never wears dresses anyway except at church. She'd cut her hair short not long before, after a trip to see her old friend Betsy the teacher at the University in Chat-tanooga, and it stood straight up on the top like a little stand of alfalfa. It made her look older somehow, making the wrinkles in her forehead kind of float out at you. I'd already got a big stack of Krispy

Kreme boxes out of the car before I noticed she was standing there with my python, Mike, wrapped around her arms. She dropped him down on the grass and said, "Dammit, Hal."

"What's the matter?" I said. I was holding about twelve boxes of doughnuts, stacked all the way up to my nose.

Ellie spit into the grass. "It's your snake, Hal. He done ate Hal Junior's favorite guinea pig, Lisa."

I looked down at Mike as he coiled himself up like a hose. There was a big lump on him that I figured must be Lisa. The lump kind of wiggled a little, but I knew there was nothing I could do.

I looked up at Ellie, who I guess you should know is about six inches taller than me, and I said, "Well, I guess we got too many animals crawling around here anyway."

She laughed at that, because she'd been telling me that same thing for years and I'd always denied it. I could hear a mockingbird somewhere up in the hackberry tree next to the house. It sounded anxious, like it was trying to remind me of something. I carried the doughnuts to the porch and then walked back toward Ellie, who was glaring at me like I was some kind of insect.

And then I did something that surprises me even now. I walked over to her and put my arms around her and pulled her close, so close my nose was rubbing against the knot in her tie and I could see the little Cub Scout bear-faces on her wide brass buttons. There was a buttermilk smell rising from her, and for a few seconds she kept her arms at her side, real stiff like a tree, with that mockingbird going crazy above us. Finally she put her arms around me, too, and we both squeezed, and I felt her body kind of loosen and soften, and I heard her sniff a little, like she was crying or something, so I got to thinking that maybe she was ready to let me come back. What a woman needs is love, I remember that old advice from the Dive Den and from Oscar and from old love songs; so I started kind of rubbing around, and I put my face up against her neck and sort of nuzzled her there, and after a little while a plane came flying over real low, so loud the ground seemed to shake. As the plane faded away Ellie went stiff again and backed a couple of inches away from me. Then she came in closer, her eyes spreading wide and shiny in a wrinkled kind of smile, and she put her pale dry lips up against my ear and spread her hands out across the sides of my head and squeezed a little. I could feel her breath hot in my ear.

"Hal—darling," she whispered. "Get your slimy hands off my ass, Hal."

I stepped back and she raised her right hand like she was about to slap me, but then she dropped it, and I noticed a tear run down her cheek. She wiped it away real fast with her forearm and tried to scowl at me.

"Dammit, Hal," she whispered. Her eyes were brimming over. "Dammit!"

"Ellie, what is it?"

"You mean you don't know?"

"Well, what I mean is—"

"What you mean is you don't even care."

"Ellie, I do." I stepped toward her.

"What you mean is, you don't care about nothing—not about me or Hal Junior or anything that really matters. What you mean is, you're just a dirty old man." And that's when she slapped me. "And that goes for Dixie Pepper, too!" And then she marched back to the house.

The Cub Scouts seemed to be in some kind of fight inside the house as I stood there with my mouth hanging open, asking myself, "What is it with her, anyway? What can I possibly do to make that woman happy?" I stacked the forty-two boxes of Krispy Kremes carefully on the front porch and headed back to the Dart, and as I drove away I glanced back toward the porch and saw Oscar and Hal Junior. They had come outside and were sitting there beside those Krispy Kremes. Hal Junior's face was puffy from crying, and Oscar had his arm around his shoulders, talking to him. Hal Junior seemed to listen closely to every word Oscar said as he wiped tears from his cheeks with the back of his hand. And even though I knew at that moment my marriage might finally be over for good, I realize now that I was too stupid to see what should've been obvious—that the only one to blame was me.

■

Anyway, the point is, you know how you start feeling responsible for every living thing that ever came along in your life, even things that don't even *know* you feel responsible for them and could care less? Like Muck the dog and Mike the python and Bart the cat, and Ellie and Hal Junior, and those guinea pigs and goats, and even Oscar, that old bastard. After I saw Hal Junior on that porch in his Cub Scout suit crying, I couldn't get it out of my mind, and I started feeling bad about every living thing I'd ever known, like somehow I had failed them all. But I also started feeling like I had to get away from them too—away from the house, the wife, the kid, the animals, away from everything.

So I drove off, not sure where I would go. Then after a little while I started thinking about Hank the goat running around loose, smashing Dixie Pepper's window and all that. And the more I thought about it, the more obsessed I got with it. It started to seem like every responsibility I had ever had in my life was embodied in that goat—in fact I started to believe that taking charge of that goat was more important than anything else in the world. I figured that the only decent thing to do was to drive out to the Pepper place and have a look around.

■

The damnedest thing was, I found Hank over at the shopping mall. I seen him out of the corner of my eye as I drove by on my way to Dixie's. He was in one of those brick boxes full of river pebbles out in the parking lot, chewing on a boxwood shrub. I bribed him out with some chocolate-covered raisins, throwing a handful of them into the back of my Dart station wagon. Hank put his front hooves up on the bumper of the Dart and started sniffing around inside. So I placed my shoulder up against his haunches and started pushing, trying to act casual about it—but of course it's not easy to act casual when you got a goat's butt in your face. After a minute I started feeling dizzy, what with the smell of that goat's ass and the hairy weight of it wiggling and pushing back against me, and the sun was like fire on the blacktop—I could see wavy patterns coming off it as I struggled with Hank, who was basically trying to sit down on me. I thought for a second I'd have to give up, but finally old Hank's legs buckled under him and he settled down, chewing on some empty Big Mac cartons that were there in the back of the Dart. With some effort I was able to get the wagon door closed, and I leaned up against it breathing hard, with sweat all over me. I looked around the parking lot, hoping to hell Mr. Bates didn't see me. Mr. Bates was head of security at the mall, and just three days earlier I'd applied for a job as night watchman. Luckily I didn't see the patrol car anywhere around, but I did see a couple of purple-haired teenage girls with safety pins in their noses. They stared at me like I'd just dropped in from the moon. After a few minutes I got my energy up and drove over to Dixie's place.

Goats: The Courtship of Dixie Pepper

IV.

Dixie Pepper didn't hear me drive up. When I got there she was covering the broken picture window with plastic and duct tape. There was a ghetto blaster radio blasting out some kind of jazz music that didn't seem to have any beat or melody or anything, and it was so loud it sounded kind of fuzzy on the high parts. Dixie was wearing a little red bikini and had her orange hair piled up real high on top of her head like cotton candy, and her skin was as red as a cooked lobster. I stood there about ten feet away under her daddy's Granny Smith apple tree, watching her stretch up high to spread that tape out over the top edge of the plastic and then bend down low to tuck in the bottom edge, and I guess I may as well admit she looked real good to me right then.

But after a couple of minutes I got kind of nervous, like a peeping Tom or something, so I walked up behind her and said, "I done caught that goat, Dixie Pepper," but still she didn't hear me. So I started saying it again and pecked her on the shoulder, and she jumped and spun around real fast, looking kind of wild for a second—scared, I think. But real quick a smile smoothed out her face and she said, "What did you say, Honey?" She was yelling it really, so I yelled back, "That goat! I captured that goat—that *goat!*"

And what she did then really surprised me. She nodded and grinned real big and kind of jumped up and down a little and started squealing, "Really? Oh, goody! Oh, goody!" Then she dropped her duct tape and grabbed me by the hand and pulled me over to my car and we started getting old Hank out, with her doing most of the work and still hollering "Oh goody, Oh goody" the whole time. I watched her bend down to grab him by the horns, pulling him up close against her red bikini chest. When he was out she took some nylon clothesline and tied him to Red's Pride of Georgia peach tree. Then she ran her jiggling red bikini self into the house, and came out with one of them expensive Japanese cameras and started taking pictures of old Hank the goat—lots of pictures. She even bent down real low to get close-ups. I was standing there kind of looking and wondering but mostly looking, and then all of a sudden she grabbed my arm in one hand and that ghetto blaster in the other and we took off real fast around the corner of the house. I felt frail and nervous and kind of confused—I just kind of tripped along behind her, trying real hard not to look at her bikini body too much, but I couldn't help it. It looked even better than a plain naked body would look. She plopped me down in a chair by the pool, her mouth running a mile a minute about I don't know what all—and the next thing I know she's sitting across from me drawing like crazy on a big sketch pad, looking up at me every now and then, smiling big white toothy smiles and saying, "Now be still Hal, honey, what you got? Ants in your pants?" and me trying to act casual, like it's no big deal. But I'm a pat of butter—I spread out any way she wants me to—why, I would've climbed a tree and jumped out if she told me to, but when she says, "Hal, why don't you be real nice for me and take off that old hot shirt," I just sit there with my mouth dangling open.

The ghetto blaster is screaming—some guy teaching himself how to play a horn. It sounds like a five-year-old making noises with a balloon. I see Dixie's long blue fingernails as they unbutton my shirt and she's smiling real big, her gums shiny and red. She drops my shirt on the concrete.

The sun is much too hot. Tickles of sweat roll out of my armpits and along my ribs while she does all kinds of sketches of me, from the front, the sides, even from behind. Then I sit in that chair feeling stiff as a turtle shell while she takes pictures of my chest and my hairy face, her body bending across me as she gets close-ups of my nose and mouth and forehead. I watch her smiley mouth and then her breasts, smooth and red and trembly under that Japanese camera she was poking in my face, and she's saying, "It's that face that I'm after, Hal. It's that face, it's perfect," and I know damn well it's not.

Then she was done, and when she pats my knee I shiver real big, one long hard shiver. I manage to get my shirt on and I see Dixie bending over the table fiddling with the camera. Right away I think about pinching her, but then I think about Tangerine behind that Coke machine and I realize I'd better get the goat back in the car and get out of there. I say, "Bye, Dixie Pepper," and she turns and blows me a kiss and I know my face is red like a schoolboy's. I take off around the house fumbling with my shirt buttons, with sweat running all over my face and chest, and right then I see Oscar. His four-by-four was backing out of Dixie's driveway, and right before it gets out on the road I see Oscar's face stick out the window, and I can *feel* those eyes poke across the yard at me. That look comes flying across the yard like a couple of darts jabbing through the air.

And it's a few minutes before I realize the goat is gone. Of course, I should've known the goat would chew his way free from that nylon clothesline. But if he did chew through it, he done a good job, because there wasn't a thread of rope left anywhere around the tree. And when Rollo Hixson finally caught up with that old goat a few days later, he claimed there wasn't any rope on it at all. He sold Hank to Dixie Pepper for next to nothing, he was so happy to get rid of him.

■

About eight days later I saw Dixie Pepper's new four-foot by four-foot pencil drawing hanging on the wall next to the banana tree outside Hallmark Cards in the Bucktooth Haven Indoor Mall.

Somehow Dixie had convinced the mall folks to let her hang some of her art on the painted plywood that covers up places where stores are supposed to be. I guess New York artists like Dixie have to take whatever space they can get.

Well, I'm here to tell you that pencil drawing was the damnedest thing I ever saw in my life. How could they allow such a thing? It made my heart kind of thump fast and my chest get tight, and I had to sit on the fake marble bench next to the fountain for a while, trying to pull myself together. I guess there's no way to say it nice, and I know for sure you'll never understand what a shock it was for me to see it, but I'll try to explain—you see, Dixie Pepper had taken half of Hank the goat, the butt half of him, and kind of welded it to the top half of a man, which was odd enough in and of itself. But what really made my legs turn to rubber was that, except for the horns on that man's head and the big muscles it had on its arms and chest, the man part of that drawing—it's mainly the face I'm talking about here—was me! I didn't even have to get up close to tell. There was no doubt at all that it was me. I know me when I see me, even from far away. It was the scariest thing I ever saw, and, as I said, it was four-feet by four-feet, hanging right there beside Hallmark Cards for everyone in Bucktooth Haven to see, with a little spotlight on it.

But that's not all. Really the worst part of it—and the part that made the ex-mayor of Chattanooga, Ham Buckley, come in and take it down with a TV camera watching—was that, back between Old Hank's legs, and right in the middle of the drawing (where you always tend to look first) was the biggest darn erection I ever saw in my life. It just jumped right out at you like you were wearing 3-D glasses or something. Dixie may as well have put a big neon sign on it saying, "Looky here kids, looky here." You could even see little veins and hairs on it, it was so lifelike. And I happen to know—being a goat man ever since I was a boy—that that penis was no *goat* penis either. Dixie Pepper put a human being penis on there, sure as I'm a man. Underneath the drawing was some words, which I guess was the title of it. It said: "Sunset Satyr Serenade."

I felt a little better about Dixie later that night when me and Karlen O'Malley looked up "satyr" in the dictionary. Knowing that a satyr was something, with a history behind it and all, made me know that at least Dixie hadn't completely flipped her lid. But still it was possible she was having something psychological going on in her mind over her daddy dying, or whatever. And I figure that a lot of people in Bucktooth Haven still see that drawing as proof that Dixie is the looniest tune in Tennessee, and I'll admit that's what I thought too, at first. The fact is, it was nothing at all like the other art she hung in the mall, which was mostly pictures of things people around here like, things like barns and flowers and kitty cats—though as I recall, seems like there was a flying pink horse with a horn sticking out of it's head, hanging next to Record Bar.

■

I guess I don't need to tell you that Dixie's half-me, half-Hank satyr was the final straw as far as Ellie was concerned. She filed papers right away, not wasting any time. She managed to get a court date only two weeks later, since Judge Fowler was a distant cousin on her father's side. And of course Marty the lawyer was off in Hawaii, now that I needed him for a change. He just sent his secretary in with a note for the judge, but I didn't pay any attention to it. In a way it didn't matter all that much. There was nothing Marty could have done anyway.

Divorce court wasn't really a court, it was just a room in a little trailer out behind the main courthouse. Ellie brought that satyr in as evidence (along with a sworn statement from Oscar saying I was out at Dixie's with my shirt off) and, for some reason, a picture of Mike the python. I didn't even pay much attention, I just let it all swim by me, even the part about them having to delay the final paperwork until Marty got back from Hawaii. But then right at the end all hell broke loose, with Oscar busting into the little courtroom, waving his arms and yelling like a madman, smelling like bourbon and looking like a werewolf, with a three-day growth of beard and grass-stained overalls. "Hey Fowler, I object, I object, I object!"

Harry Fowler didn't even bother calling in a bailiff or policeman or anything, he just stood up and grabbed Oscar by the bib of his overalls and shoved him out the door of the trailer and said, "Oscar McNairy, if you do that again I'm holding you in contempt," and he slammed the door and locked it right in Oscar's objecting face.

But what surprised me even more was how, the following week, when it looked like I was going to live all alone in that little room above Chuckie's store for the rest of my life, Oscar shows up with his truck full of my animals. Bart the cat, Mike the python, a whole bunch of guinea pigs, some gerbils, a tank full of tropical fish, two nanny goats—all the animals I had left.

"She wants you to have 'em," says Oscar. He put his hand on my shoulder, real solemn like at a funeral. "We both thought it would be best that you have 'em."

And right then I thought about Muck, the Army dog. I thought about his eyes, those special dog eyes that could almost talk to you, and how he finally went blind and died. He had quite a stare, you know. He could stare right through you, right into the inside part of you.

■

I saw Dixie Pepper a few times after that, in places like the hardware store and drugstore, but I couldn't bring myself to talk to her. I felt like a schoolboy, tongue-tied and embarrassed by the mere sight of her, and she just waltzed around like princesses do in fairy tales, oozing out beauty like some kind of gas, going on with her business, like nothing had even happened between us.

One time, when I was wandering through the produce section of the new grocery store over near the mall, Dixie just suddenly appeared right in front of me, magically, as though she had crawled out from under one of them big pyramids of apples. She didn't even say hello or anything like that, she just said, "Hal, where do you reckon they keep the garlic?"

My mouth hung open like it had sprung a hinge, and finally I mumbled something like, "Hell, Dixie, I wouldn't know a garlic if it crawled up my nose."

And that was that.

Of course, I guess it was best that Dixie and I stayed away from each other. What puzzled me, though, was that Oscar started hanging around the Pepper place all of a sudden. After my divorce, I drove by the Pepper place a bunch of times on my way to the mall, and it seemed like Oscar's four-by-four was just about always parked there, right beside Red Pepper's Granny Smith apple tree. And in my opinion, Oscar McNairy had no business being anywhere near a woman like Dixie Pepper.

V.

When Marty the lawyer got back from Hawaii, he pushed the paperwork through and the divorce was official, so I gave him a call. "Why does anybody need marriage?" I said to Marty as a summing up kind of thing. "I mean, what good is marriage when you can join the Army and blow things up? Hell, you blow things up all the time in the Army, big mushroom explosions like you wouldn't believe, but the problem is, you end up coming back home and getting married anyway, kind of accidentally, like falling buck naked into a vat of glue, and you end up settling down and getting fat and tending all the little animals with no light at the end of the tunnel. But still you've got the quarry! Still you can blow things up!"

"Blow it up, Hal," says Marty. "You're a free man."

"Yep," I said. "Blow it up! I'm a free man."

"Hot dang," says Marty.

"Hot dang," I said back. "Except of course I ain't got the quarry no more, Marty. I ain't even got no job."

There I was in my new Salvation Army easy chair, with my new phone, and my new self, by the grimy window in my new home above Chuckie's store, with a white patch of sunlight on my lap and Bart the cat slinking around, and I don't have a dang thing to do. It's like life's over. Suddenly it felt like I'd been there before, in exactly that same place—in that chair by that window with that same beam of sunlight. The cat jumped up on my lap into the sunlight and dug his claws in just so I could feel the sharpness, without cutting in deep, and that's when it happened—the thing I didn't want to get in my mind got in there anyway. It was Hal Junior, my eight-year-old son, and I could feel something hard rise in my throat and I thought maybe I might cry, so I put the phone on the receiver without even saying good-bye to Marty the lawyer, who may have already hung up for all I knew, and I sat very still, watching the evening sunshine come through the window. After a while Mike the python emerged from a pile of laundry and slithered toward me; I reached down and picked him up, wrapping him around my shoulders, and he pulled in snug around me. I fell asleep like that, and when I awoke it was dark outside. The cat was on my lap and the python on my shoulders, exactly as before. I managed to reach my hip flask and take a swallow without disturbing the animals. I turned on the TV with the remote control, and I'm thinking: so this is it. This is what I wanted. This is how the marriage ends, right here, just like this.

■

The last time I saw Oscar McNairy was later that same night. Again I woke up sitting in my chair with Mike the python wrapped around my neck, in that trance that reptiles go into. The cat had slipped away somewhere, and the TV was still on. It was showing close-up pictures of dogwood blossoms and playing "The Star Spangled Banner." I started thinking, "Hell, I can sing if I want to, I'm king of this manor." So I started singing about the twilight's last gleaming and bombs bursting in air, and I felt better somehow, I felt happy. And right then, right when the TV picture blipped off into fuzz, the telephone rang.

It was Dixie Pepper. She started in real fast about how she couldn't talk about it on the phone, but if I was ever in my life a friend to Oscar McNairy and her poor dead daddy Red Pepper I'd better get over to her place right away and never say a word about it to anybody. She hung up. I sat there with that phone to my ear and Mike around my neck and I stared at the fuzzy TV screen until the phone started beeping real loud. Then I dropped Mike on the bed and took off.

■

Dixie met me out in the front yard next to one of Red's Bartlett pear trees. There was no moon. I could see her face float pale orange in the dark every time she took a draw on her cigarette.

"I guess it's silly to have you come over here, Hal," she said.

"What is it, Dixie?"

"It's Oscar." There was a long pause. "In the pool." She looked

105

away, and somehow I knew right away what had happened. But I couldn't speak.

Dixie drew hard on her cigarette. "I thought it might be best," she said, "to get him out before—well, you know." Her voice was like tin cans. She lit another cigarette with the butt of the first one, and I'm standing there looking past her, at the big picture window. She still didn't have it fixed, and the plastic had come off. It looked like it had fallen inside, into the living room, as if somebody had leaned on it too hard.

We walked around the side of the house to the pool. It was lit by blue lights under the water and big white lights on poles around the edges. It was a damn nice pool, the deluxe model built by Pools Unlimited down on Buckton Pike near the sewage treatment plant. She must've paid a bundle for it. Her daddy Red would turn over in his grave.

Oscar looked like a giant lump of wax, floating face down in the shallow end. Dixie was standing behind me and I turned toward her. She had on her red bikini, but she seemed like a little plastic doll the way her shoulders hunched down and her arms folded across her chest. Her orange hair was wet, hanging in strands down to her shoulders.

"How come he's out there, Dixie Pepper?" She tried not to look at me but she couldn't help it. Her eyes were round like silver dollars.

"Why, he must've snuck in," she said. "You know, for a swim in the pool."

I saw her lower lip start to quiver.

"Well, I guess so," I said. "For a swim." We both turned toward Oscar, floating in that still, blue water, his bare skin kind of pale and splotchy. His butt was as white as a hunk of ivory. I stood there thinking how there's no dignity in death, there never has been. I've always said Oscar was like a daddy to me, and I still say that even now, but at that moment he sure didn't seem even close to one. Just because he was my real daddy's friend, just because he took me to a few ball games and on a few fishing trips, just because he let me borrow his truck a few times, just because he showed me what a condom was, just because he claimed he kept me out of trouble when trouble was all there was to get in, just because he came over and fixed bad light fixtures and unclogged drains for my momma, just because he objected to every goddamn thing I ever tried to do in my whole life and tried to undermine even my own crumbling marriage—just because of all that, does that mean he was a daddy to me? That he was more than just some guy who happened to live at a place near mine?

Dixie Pepper was standing there in her red bikini, about to cry, her makeup kind of floating above her face it was so thick, and after a while I said, "I guess he died happy, then, don't you think?"

Her eyes were kind of blank, like she didn't quite understand the question. "Yeah," she said, "I guess so."

I could hear cicada bugs making long circular drawling sounds in the trees behind the pool. Dixie then looked at me with a look that said a whole lot, stuff I didn't even want to know for sure.

Then I just had to ask.

"Dixie," I says. "I don't get it." Oscar looked like a log there in the shallow end. "An old guy like that, a lady like you, in her prime. I just don't get it at all."

She stared at my eyes, and the expression that came across her face right then was spooky to see. It was like her face didn't know which emotion to have, so it flipped from one to another real fast and finally settled on a combination of them all.

Finally she said, "I see what you're thinking, Hal. But it's not that. It's not that at all."

We both gazed at the pool for a while, at the little tiny ripples in it.

"Of course, it's really no use, is it?" she said. "No matter what I say, you'll go on thinking what you're thinking. I can't change it." She paused, lit another cigarette, and exhaled like a long sigh. "What if I told you I loved him? Would that change anything?" She laughed and drew in real hard on the cigarette. "Or what if I told you I hate him? How about that? What if I said he was like a father to me? Or that he was from the moon?"

She laughed again and blew smoke into the air between us. I didn't know what to say. I walked a few feet away and watched the night, like a wall beyond the lights of the pool. After a couple of minutes she came up beside me and said, "What if I told you this, Hal." She put her face near my ear and lowered her voice. "What if I told you he tried to rape me?"

I turned and looked straight into her eyes for maybe the first time ever in my life. Then I looked up at the moths swarming around the lights of the pool, blind like old Muck, and Dixie said, "Don't you see? Don't you see that no matter what I say, I can't change things? I can't change whatever is in your mind."

Dixie walked to the edge of the pool and looked at Oscar's body. "I've been a target all my life," she said in a sad, soft way, like she was talking to the air. "Since before Daddy died, people's been after me. My fool daddy saw to that."

Then she turned toward me and let out a sharp, angry laugh and said, "It started with you, Hal."

"Now hold on, Dixie—"

"I always had this body, and now I got some money, too. That makes me just about perfect, don't it? I'm just a big old pretty piece of pie. And we all know that when a woman finally gets herself a piece of the pie, she can't just have it like a man does. No, she can't have it. She can't have it because every guy for miles around figures

108

it's his God-given duty to come sniffing around, poking his sticky fingers in it."

"Now Dixie Pepper," I said, "I don't think that way about you."

She laughed again and said, "The hell you don't!" And I could see tears in her eyes. I reached for her shoulder, trying to touch her gently in a reassuring way, but it didn't come out right. She drew back from me, glaring, so I walked away from her and sat on the edge of the diving board.

"And what if it were all true," I heard her say. "What if everything you think about me and that old man were really true? What then?"

I stared at the pebbles in the concrete.

"Maybe it is true, Hal. In fact, I'll just say so. Here goes, you listening? It's true! Everything you think about me and that old man is true. Did you hear that, Hal? Now you tell me—why can't you accept a notion like that? Why would you be so bothered by the idea of a little tenderness between two people?"

I could feel her eyes on me. Clearly she was expecting an answer, but I couldn't say anything. I stood up and turned to face Oscar.

"The fact is," she said, "he was a friend." Her voice was calm now, and when I turned and looked into her eyes, she looked sadder than any human being I've ever seen, before or since.

"There's no comfort in life," she said. "The thing is, why? Why can't a woman have a little comfort in life?"

"Comfort?" I said. I looked around and held my arms out. "You ain't got comfort?" And instantly I felt like the world's biggest jackass.

She laughed and drew hard on her cigarette. Then she laughed harder, a kind of coughing laugh with smoke coming out of her nose. And it was then that I noticed her artist's easel, set up at the other end of the pool. There was a human figure on it, the outline of a man.

Dixie laughed a little more, then sighed the last of the smoke from

109

her lungs. She threw her cigarette into the pool, curled up on a lawn chair, and was quiet.

There was nothing to say. She seemed small, curled there on the chair like a cat. And for a moment I thought that I didn't know her at all. I started thinking that maybe I've never really seen what's been right in front of me all my life. Me, Oscar, Chuckie, Marty the lawyer—it could be we're all like old Muck the dog, staring at the fireball; stumbling along in the light from all the explosions we've made for ourselves; tripping over clear and simple things simply because we've been looking so hard for those very things that we can't see them for what they really are.

I watched the moths—it seemed like millions were swarming the lights around the pool. I watched a bat dive blind into that moth-filled light and feast there, and I was struck with the idea that maybe the way the world has always worked is no good anymore. Maybe the way things really are is impossible to know as long as we keep believing what we've always believed and acting the way we've always acted.

Dixie stayed curled up on the chair, hiding her face in her arms. I knew the conversation was over. I called an ambulance for Oscar and then went home to my room.

■

I didn't go to the funeral. Oscar never was real big on ceremonies anyway. The Chattanooga paper said Oscar was found in his swim trunks in a Bucktooth Haven swimming pool. That's pretty much all it said, in a little one paragraph thing stuck down at the bottom of a movie review. Later they ran a real obituary but I didn't read it, because I knew it or anything else couldn't tell his life the way it needed to be told. I guess Dixie slipped a pair of Red's shorts on

Oscar before the Bucktooth Haven Rescue Squad got there—probably those khaki ones Red always used to wear to the church picnics. Getting them on Oscar was probably pretty easy to do, since he was floating real well, there in the shallow end. When I went to the doctor to get a checkup, that boy doctor, Alvin Hixson, told me he had lunch with the guy who did Oscar's autopsy. He said Oscar had a heart attack, he didn't drown. He said Oscar died with a smile on his face, a happy man. He winked when he said it.

I stared at him. "What the hell you trying to say, boy?" I said to Alvin Hixson.

He looked at me kind of sheepish for a minute and said, "Nothing, Hal, never mind. I didn't mean nothing by it."

Then he stuck a stethoscope up against my chest and listened real close, and we didn't say anything else about it.

The Sanctuary

The younger boys played tag among rows of cinder blocks stacked on the lawn of the church. The older ones stayed to themselves. Barnes threw a baseball against the side of the old sanctuary, catching it on the rebound. White flakes of paint dusted the grass with each throw. Men were working inside the condemned building, prying salvageable lumber from the walls and hammering out old nails. A dusty smell came from the broken windows.

"Wake up, Gregory, you lard-licker," Barnes said.

Gregory was stretched out on one of the plywood picnic tables beside the gully that ran behind the church. He stared into the willow branches above him.

"Lard-licker," Barnes repeated. "Fat-boy." Gregory turned his head from Barnes and covered his eyes with his arm. Barnes, Gregory, and Ian were the oldest boys on the team, and Barnes was always bugging everybody else.

"Hey Fat-boy," Barnes said again, grinning. He threw the baseball at Gregory and it bounced off his belly, rolling into the gully. Gregory rose to a sitting position, his soft face pulling tight as he rubbed his belly. "Not nice, Barnes!" Barnes ran toward the front of the sanctuary.

Ian crouched in weeds beside the sanctuary's front steps, in the corner where the staircase joined the wooden building. He was pulling bagworm pods from one of the shrubs, stacking them in neat piles beside the stone foundation. The pods were made of dried leaves, and inside each pod was a shiny green worm. He made three pyramids of about twenty pods each.

"Ian! Hey Ian!" Barnes threw his ball glove at Ian, but it hit the shrub and fell to the grass. "Come on, man, what're you doing?"

"Nothing." Ian stayed in his crouch, turning his back toward Barnes.

Barnes rubbed his shoes in the grass and gazed across the gravel lot as Coach's blue sedan rumbled in, sending a cloud of dust across the church lawn. The sweaty boys at the cinder blocks waved their arms as dust sprinkled their faces. Coach crawled from the car, his twisted left leg coiling behind him like a spring. He pushed the door shut with his cane. An olive-skinned boy with a beaked chin slipped from the passenger's seat, his eyes scanning the ground. He kicked up dust with his boots.

"Man, you won't believe who came with Coach," said Barnes. "Dean Forester, from school. An eighth-grader."

Ian pulled more pods from the shrub. "So?"

"He got expelled last week. Punched a teacher or something." Barnes spit into the bushes and grinned. "He ain't no church boy, not by a long shot."

Ian ran his hand across his forehead and squinted up at the sky. He took another pod from the shrub, holding it between his thumbs. "Coach thinks baseball will change the world," he said. He squeezed the pod in the middle, watching the worm ooze out at both ends.

Barnes stepped closer and crouched with Ian beside the concrete staircase. He looked at the pods. "What are those?"

Ian shrugged. "Little houses." He plucked another swollen pod from the bush and squeezed. "Little places to hide."

Barnes pulled his T-shirt off and wiped his face with it. He took the oozing pod from Ian and held it against the sky. "It's nothing but slime," said Barnes. "Fat-boy Gregory slime." Barnes took a pod from the top of a pyramid and squeezed. "No—it's dog dicks. Fat-boy dog dicks." They both laughed.

A wheezing sound came from somewhere above them. "Preacher!" Ian whispered. Barnes took a deep breath, his skin tightening across his ribs. The preacher quivered up the steps in a slow sway, high above the crouching boys. At the landing he turned toward the iron rail, his chest rising and falling. Ian ran his eyes up the hairless pink legs. They expanded like cones of gelatin, bulging into the tan cuffs of his Bermuda shorts. The preacher held a crowbar in his right hand. "Afternoon boys," he said, raising the crowbar to his forehead, then down again.

"Afternoon, Reverend Murray," said Barnes, loudly. "A fine day sir, a very fine day. For enjoying God's creation, that is."

The preacher raised the crowbar toward the sky, moving it in an arc. His T-shirt rode up above his navel and the smooth flesh of his belly arched out, gummy and pink. A wide baby face, pasty with sweat, floated high above the belly. "Where two or more are gathered," he said, "there am I, boys, there am I." The preacher ran his left hand across his scalp, his breath sliding from his chest like sandpaper as he winked down at the boys.

Ian looked at Barnes. "God's creation," he whispered. They both laughed.

Gregory tramped into the bushes and looked up. "Hello, Reverend Murray," he said. The preacher stuck a finger in his ear and rolled his head back, looking at the sky.

Gregory turned to the two boys crouching in the weeds. "You guys better come right now; Coach is here." He stepped closer, his eyes widening. "What're you guys doing, anyway?"

"None of your damn business," said Barnes. Barnes stood and brushed his blond hair from his eyes. "Fat-boy."

Gregory hunched his shoulders. "Quiet," he whispered. "What if the preacher hears?" There was a loud beeping noise, and Gregory looked up again. The preacher had his back to them now, his hand over his right ear. The sanctuary door creaked open.

"He can't hear shit," said Barnes.

"That's not nice, Barnes."

"So?"

Gregory giggled, his face sweaty and red. He put his tennis shoe against Barnes' thigh and pushed, and Barnes chased him out of the bushes. Ian emerged as Barnes jumped on Gregory's back. He could hear Gregory giggling and Barnes giggling, too. Barnes clung to Gregory's back, muttering something in his ear, and Gregory staggered across the grass. Some of the younger boys gathered around.

Then the olive-skinned boy appeared. He leaned against a stack of gray cinder blocks. Barnes looked up and stopped giggling and started kicking at the backs of Gregory's knees. Gregory twirled and staggered in a wide loop. He seemed to bounce when he finally hit the ground. The kids laughed, and the olive-skinned boy laughed, too. Gregory was on his belly with Barnes astride his back, and Barnes began hitting him hard on the arms with his fists. Gregory stopped giggling and began yelling, his face hot crimson with bits of dried grass stuck to his cheeks. At last he rolled over, throwing Barnes to the ground.

Ian saw Coach inching out from behind the cinder blocks, a coffee can in his right hand. With the cane he crawled like a spider. His thin right cheek bulged out. "Boys!" he said. His lips didn't move. "Boys!" The boys grew quiet and Coach spit something into the coffee can.

"Tobacco spit," whispered the olive-skinned boy. The boy stood now beside Ian. Ian looked at the boy's sunken cheek, the way it hollowed below the sharp bone of his eye socket.

"No," said Ian. "Prunes. Prune pits."

The boy turned away.

Barnes rose to his knees in the grass while Coach put the rubber tip of his cane against Gregory's chest. "Boys, boys," he said, his lips thin and still. "We're all temples of God, all of us." The cane rose and fell with Gregory's breath. Some of the boys whispered to each other. "Now you two, you should be ashamed. After all, the Bible says love one another, don't it?" The cane moved from the chest along the crest of the belly to the navel. "Don't it?" He smiled, his gums rubbing together. "Though of course, the woman at the well—"

Gregory giggled.

"Is it all that funny?"

"It tickles, Coach." Gregory rolled across the grass and the younger boys began laughing. "Sorry, Coach."

Coach turned toward Barnes. "Barnes, bring the bats and balls from my car."

Barnes stood. "Come on, Fat-boy," he whispered. The other boys turned toward the ball field.

"But first," said Coach. "First let me tell you boys a little story." The boys stopped and turned back toward Coach. He set the coffee can on the ground and leaned forward, both hands on the cane. Gray stubble covered his chin. He stared at the cinder blocks, his eyes tiny behind thick horn-rimmed glasses.

Several of the boys flopped to the grass but Ian slipped away, trotting along a lane of cinder blocks toward the gully. Coach's voice followed, seeming to drift above him in the hot air. "Once Zel Miller had this cow, see? It was a good cow too, best at the fair. Milk cow."

The footbridge that led across the gully to the ball field was covered with red mud. Ian stood beside the footbridge and looked down toward the stream. He could still hear Coach's lazy voice, far away now. "That cow was a good cow," said Coach. "But it had problems. People problems, mostly. That's howcome the milk just wouldn't flow. Some people expect milk no matter what, but it just won't come some days. So Zel, he got himself a old Victrola. You boys know what a Victrola is?"

Ian climbed down the gully wall to the streambed. Heavy rains had caused red hunks of earth to slide down the sides of the gully, and though the hunks were drying out, there was plenty of water in the stream. The sound of Coach's voice was gone now. There was only the hissing of the water and the hum of insects. Ian stooped to watch a water strider scoot across a pool. The strider's legs made tiny indentations in the water's smooth surface. Ian stirred up muck from the bottom of the pool with a stick, watching the strider bounce over the muddy ripples.

"What you gonna be when you grow up?" someone said.

Ian's shoulders twitched. He dropped the stick and stood quick and turned to see the olive-skinned boy behind him, kicking his boot against a rock embedded in mud. The boy picked up the rock and threw it across the gully, into mud on the other side.

"What did you say?" Ian asked.

"I said, what you gonna be? You know, when you grow up."

Ian's eyebrow rose, wrinkling his forehead. He looked closely at the boy. The boy was several inches taller than Ian.

"Is your name Dean?"

The boy nodded.

"You're an eighth-grader."

"Yeah. So."

Ian reached for a rock. "I'm gonna be a doctor," said Ian. He threw the rock into the stream. The boy threw a rock, too, skimming it off the water to the other side of the gully.

"Well, what about you, Dean? What you gonna be?"

The boy bent for another rock. He skimmed it too, then bent for another, throwing it high in the air. It plopped into mud on the other side. "Nothing," he said. He kicked at a rock with his boot. "Just never mind." The boy walked to the shade of the footbridge and sat on an old tire at the edge of the water, his boots sinking into mud. He laughed for a second and then was quiet.

Ian shrugged. He walked to a pool of clear water a few feet away. A crayfish emerged from beneath a submerged rock, scuttling across dead leaves at the bottom of the shallow pool. Ian poked a stick at the crayfish and the crayfish fought it, tapping with its front claws. Ian scooted around the pool, trying to avoid the sun's glare off the water. He heard the rumble of his teammates crossing the footbridge as the crayfish backed under a lip of rock, then lunged out at the stick. Ian looked up as Coach shuffled along, his cane, arms, and good leg fluttering before him. Behind Coach came Barnes, with his left leg twisted beneath him, using a ball bat for a cane. He poked his cheek out with his tongue and spit off the bridge into the water; then he looked at Ian and grinned, pointing his thumb at Coach. Gregory walked red-faced behind Barnes, dragging the canvas bat-sack and snickering into the palm of his hand. "And you know, boys," Coach said, "sometimes not even God can save a bleeding cow. Not even God." His voice faded away as he led the boys to the ball field.

Ian squatted again by the pool, poking the crayfish with the stick.

"Well, are you going with them or what?" The olive-skinned boy still sat on the muddy tire.

"Maybe," said Ian. "Maybe not."

The olive-skinned boy lit a cigarette and sighed out a stream of blue smoke. The smoke floated around his head and curled up under the footbridge.

Footsteps pounded across the bridge, and the boy smashed the cigarette in the mud. The two boys watched as Barnes climbed down into the gully. "That crippled old weasel," Barnes said, scratching his crotch. "Boys do this, boys do that. Don't do this, don't do that. The cow! The cow!" Barnes put his muddy red sneaker on the tire beside Dean and leaned forward, one elbow on his knee. "Why put up with that, hey Dean? Why put up with bull like that? Why not just say screw 'em? You know what I mean?" Dean stood and walked toward the pool where Ian was. "Man, I say screw 'em," said Barnes. He plodded along behind Dean, his shoes making a sucking sound in the mud. "Yeah, you know what I mean. Screw 'em." He stopped and poked his fists in his pockets. "Say, Dean, how about fronting me a smoke, man."

"How about shutting your foul mouth," said Dean. He slung his hair back with a twist of his neck.

"Since when do you smoke, Barnes?" said Ian, working the crayfish with the stick. He didn't look up from the pool.

"What do you mean, oatmeal-brain?" Barnes said. He laughed. "What are they, man? Luckies?"

Dean held the pack of cigarettes toward Ian, but Ian ignored him. Barnes stood behind Dean, stretching his neck forward. "Hey, I'll have one."

Dean put a cigarette in his own mouth and lit it with a match, then held the pack over his shoulder to Barnes. "Thanks, man," said Barnes. He held the unlit cigarette in his lips.

"Hey, you guys!" The boys turned. Gregory sat on the footbridge, his legs dangling over the edge. "Are those cigarettes?" he said. "Real cigarettes? You guys better not let Coach catch you with cigarettes."

"Shut up, Fat-boy," said Barnes.

"I'm just telling you. Besides, Coach says you better get to practice now or you're in big trouble." Barnes threw a lump of mud at Gregory and he scurried to his feet, heading back to the ball field. "I'll kick your butt if you tell," Barnes yelled after him. "Screw 'em," he said.

"I said shut your foul mouth," Dean said to Barnes. Dean squatted beside the pool and watched as the crayfish attacked the stick. Ian pulled it up but the crayfish turned loose at the surface. Dean took a long draw on his cigarette. He sighed again and looked up at the footbridge. "What's wrong with this Coach guy, anyway?" he said after a while. "His leg, I mean."

Ian shrugged. "It's his spinal cord."

"A whore kicked him down a staircase," said Barnes, the cigarette bouncing in his mouth. He laughed with his lips tight around the unlit cigarette. "Half his pecker's gone too."

"Naw," said Dean.

"It's true."

"Shut your face, Barnes," Ian said, holding the wet stick above the water. Ian stood and turned toward Barnes. "I mean it." Dean grinned and blew smoke into the air between the two boys, and Ian squatted down beside the pool again.

"Well, it's true."

"It is not," said Ian. "He was injured in the war. Ran under fire into a Jap bunker."

"He did not!"

"Did too."

121

"Did not."

Dean coughed. "Either way," said Dean, "it's a dumb thing to let happen to yourself." Blue smoke streamed from his nose and wrapped around his head.

Ian wiped his forearm across his face and pulled the stick out of the water. The crayfish clung to the end of the stick. Its translucent body looked crisp in the sun.

"My daddy says Coach is a queer," said Barnes. He stepped forward and kicked the crayfish from the stick. The boys watched the crayfish fly into the air, into blue sky.

Ian grabbed Barnes by the arm. "You got a problem?" said Ian. Barnes looked away, red rising in his cheeks. He looked at Dean and puffed his chest with air. Then he dropped the unlit cigarette, pointing to the footbridge. "Preacher!" he whispered. The three boys turned toward the bridge.

"Afternoon, boys," said the preacher. "It's lunchtime." He moved across the sagging footbridge. He had a stained paper bag in one hand and the crowbar in the other.

"Afternoon, Reverend Murray," said Barnes.

The preacher stopped and swung toward them, his mouth pink and sagging. "Boys, let me tell you something about that old sanctuary," he said. He held the crowbar at arm's length and looked at it, then at the boys. "We're tearing it down, you know. But the fact is, tearing down or building up—it doesn't matter. You know why?" He winked at them. "Because it's all the work of the Lord, that's why." He dropped the bag and slapped at a mosquito.

"That's right," said Barnes. "God's work."

"Is practice already over?" The preacher cupped his ear with his free hand and squinted at the boys.

"Not yet," said Barnes. "No." He shook his head.

"Well, then. I'll watch." The preacher bent, sweat dripping from his nose as he stretched for the lunch bag. Then he swung around toward the ball field.

Dean flipped his cigarette butt into the stream. "Come on, guys," he said. "Let's play ball." They climbed from the gully, crossed the bridge, and followed a path beneath scraggly, twisted oaks to the ball field.

■

A tiny, freckled boy was at bat when they arrived. Gregory was on the pitcher's mound and Coach stood behind him, beside a bucket of baseballs. "Ian," said Coach. "Center field. Barnes, take right." The two boys trotted to the outfield, leaving Dean standing beside the first-base line, his hands stuffed in his pockets. Coach put both hands on his cane and leaned toward Dean, his eyes tiny behind his thick glasses. Then he extended his hand. "Hand 'em over, boy," he said.

Dean shuffled across the infield and put the pack of cigarettes in Coach's fingers, and Coach's lips spread back in a brown, gummy smile. "Dean," he said. "You should know better."

Gregory stood picking his nose, grinning at Dean.

"Boys," said Coach to the team. "Everything is seen. Everything. Even the fall of a sparrow is seen." Gregory stepped behind Coach and started flapping his arms like a bird.

"Take the mitt, Dean," said Coach.

Dean turned away. He saw the preacher sitting behind the rusty chicken-wire backstop, his body wedged against a tree. The folds of the preacher's neck stretched taut as he stared into the limbs of the tree, a sandwich rising to his mouth. His neck quivered as he swallowed.

Dean found the catcher's mitt and walked to home plate. Baseballs were scattered around the backstop. The freckled kid with the bat looked at Dean. "My name's Samuel," he said. Dean stared past him at Gregory. "That's *Samuel*," the boy said. "S-a-m-u-e-l. Samuel."

"Samuel," said Dean. He stared at Gregory.

"I got a glass eye," said Samuel.

"Yeah sure," said Dean. "Shut up, Samuel."

Gregory leaned forward with both hands behind his back, then wound up and threw. The ball hit dust three feet in front of the plate. "Ease up," Coach said to Gregory.

Dean scooped up the ball and threw it, hard. Gregory ducked as the ball landed square in his glove. "Hey," said Gregory. "Watch it." He glanced back at Coach, then threw again, a slow looping pitch. Samuel swung under it, hitting a high foul ball. Dean ran for the ball, squinting into the sun. It hit the dirt in front of him.

"What's wrong, Dean," said Coach. "Got smoke in your eyes?"

"Yeah, smoke," said Gregory. "He's got smoke in his eyes!" Dean tucked the mitt under his arm and turned away, rubbing the baseball with both hands.

"Forget it, Dean," said Coach. Dean turned and threw the ball back at Gregory, hard, hitting his shoulder.

"Yeah," said Dean. "Smoke."

The preacher snored behind the backstop. The snores lifted in the hot air and fluttered across the field, but nobody laughed. Coach dug his cane into the dust and spit something into the coffee can at his feet. "Sammy," he said, "take the field. Dean, grab a bat. Let's see what you can do with a bat."

Dean sized up the bats. He looked at the preacher behind the chicken wire, his neck stretched, his nose pointing straight up. The top of his head rested against the tree trunk and his mouth hung open, his nostrils vibrating with each breath.

Dean rubbed some dust on his hands and took three practice

swings. "Blast him one, Deano," yelled Barnes. "Coming right back to the mound, Fat-boy, right back to the mound."

Dean spit in his hands, stepped to the plate, and pointed the bat at Gregory. "In your face," Dean said, kicking dust across the plate. Coach leaned back on his coiled leg and twisted toward the boys in the field. "Boys," he said, "how about a little chatter out there." The boys in the infield began muttering in a monotonous drone. Gregory wound up and let the ball fly and the boys yelled "Swing!" and Dean swung hard. The ball lined straight and fast at Gregory, and Gregory ducked. The ball flew by him and caught Coach square in the temple. Dean saw the head snap back and the tangled limbs flutter in the air. He heard the thin body flop to the dust with a puffing noise. He saw Gregory roll off the mound. The boys laughed, and then grew quiet. Dean heard a strangled snore from behind the backstop.

The boys began gathering around Coach, and Gregory sat up in the dust.

"My shoulder," Gregory said, rubbing his collarbone.

"You ducked, Gregory," said Barnes. "I ought to kick your fat butt, you coward."

Ian squatted beside Coach. He ran his finger along the purple knot already forming on Coach's left temple. Coach's body twitched and Ian jumped back. Then he put his hand on Coach's wrist.

"What is it?" somebody said.

Ian stared at his own shadow. "I reckon he's dead," said Ian. "Or at least—he *could* be dead. It's possible."

"Anything's possible."

"He sure looks dead."

Somebody laughed. "He always looks dead."

"That's not nice."

"Shut up," said Ian. "Everybody shut up."

125

"Man! Look at those things in the coffee can."

"Oh, Jesus. Big brown boogers. Mouth boogers."

Somebody laughed. "He ain't dead."

"Somebody better do something," said Gregory.

"Shut your fat mouth," said Barnes. "*You're* the one that ducked! You caused it!"

"He ain't moving. Hey *Coach!* Wake up, Coach."

"Somebody get the preacher."

"Preacher's dead too." The boys laughed.

"Barnes, get the preacher," said Ian. Ian reached into Coach's shirt pocket. He pulled out the cigarettes and two prunes wrapped in plastic. "Go, Barnes."

Barnes turned toward the backstop. Dean stood at home plate, leaning on the bat. He dropped the bat and turned away when Barnes walked near him. "You're crying," said Barnes. "Are you crying?"

Ian still knelt by Coach. "Hey Reverend Murray, wake up," he yelled. More snores drifted in the air. "Barnes! Go wake up the preacher."

Barnes picked up the bat and tapped it against home plate, watching the dust bounce with each tap. Dean stood a few feet away, looking into the woods.

"Dammit, Barnes," said Ian. Ian pushed through the crowd of boys and ran around the backstop. He stood over the snoring preacher, looking into his mouth. His tongue was coated with a white paste. "Mr. Murray." Ian shook the preacher's shoulder. "Mr. Murray."

"Afternoon, boys," the preacher said to Ian. He rubbed his hand across his eyes and licked his lips.

"Coach is dead or something, Mr. Murray."

"Huh?"

126

"It's Coach. He seems dead, sort of." Ian watched the preacher's eyes. *"Dead,"* he said, pointing. *"Coach."*

Ian stooped in weeds beside the backstop as the preacher rolled to his knees. The preacher placed one foot on the ground and grasped the tree trunk with his right arm. He took the crowbar in his free hand and hooked it into the tree, pulling himself to his feet. He ran around the backstop toward the group of boys. "Stand back, boys," he said, waving the crowbar. "Get behind the backstop, out of the way." The boys scattered across the infield as the preacher slid to his knees beside Coach, dust puffing into the faces of both men. The preacher put his hand to Coach's wrist. "Ian," he yelled. "Run to the sanctuary. Call an ambulance."

Ian squatted in the weeds, flipping a dandelion with his finger. "Huh?" he said, looking up. White seeds drifted around him. "The sanctuary?"

"Run, boy!" The preacher began loosening Coach's shirt.

The boys watched as Ian ran to the edge of the woods. Then they saw him stop beside Dean and put his arm across Dean's shoulders. Dean hunched over like an old man. He dropped to his knees and Ian knelt next to him, talking to him, bending low to look straight into his eyes.

"Hurry, Ian," yelled Gregory, but Ian kept talking to Dean. Dean's body was shaking. The boys could hear noises coming from him. Finally Dean and Ian stood and walked slowly into the woods toward the sanctuary. "Hurry!" yelled Gregory. Gregory pushed his face against the chicken-wire backstop, the wire pressing into the flesh of his forehead. Barnes walked up behind Gregory and kicked the backs of his knees. "Shut up, Fat-boy." Barnes jumped on Gregory's back and locked his arms around his neck, and Gregory stepped backward and spun around, trying to sling Barnes off. He spun around and around, but Barnes hung on. He giggled, spinning harder, his face covered in sweat. The younger boys gathered around, laughing at Gregory. The pattern of the chicken wire could be seen in his skin. "Lard-licker," said Barnes. Barnes' arms slid up under Gregory's chin, forcing his face upward. Gregory kept giggling, a tear trickling from the corner of his eye. "Stop," he said. He kept spinning and spinning, and Barnes' feet left the ground. "Lard-licking coward," said Barnes. "Ducking-down lard-licking coward." Tears and sweat made Gregory's face shine. He giggled and frowned and spun around. "Stop," he said, his face twisted and red. "Stop."

Training to Be an Astronaut

When Father left me standing on the roof of the new house, three stories off the ground, I quickly realized that this was another opportunity for some astronaut training. Why, I asked myself, should I waste my time nailing shingles to a roof? After all, wasn't Neil Armstrong himself out there somewhere, at that very moment, practicing for his heroic trip to the moon? And hadn't he been preparing, in some form or fashion, since he was a child? Because the fact is, training to be an astronaut is a state of mind— you have to be constantly training, constantly preparing yourself, even if you're still just a lonely high schooler lost, as I was then, in the clay-spattered hills of East Tennessee.

Here are the most important rules of the astronaut corps—keep your head clear, keep your sights focused, and keep calm no matter how tough things get. That's why astronauts have electrodes all over their bodies. Mission Control monitors their vital signs constantly, because an astronaut has to remain calm in tough situations.

So I scooted as close as I could to the edge of the roof and forced

Brian Griffin

myself to stand erect, inching forward until my toes were hanging over the eave; then I closed my eyes, extended my arms to either side, and focused on slowing my heartbeat.

I've been working on staying calm for years, so I've gotten to be pretty good at it. Vital signs are difficult to control, though. In my eleventh grade English class there was a girl named Colleen who sat in front of me. She had big eyes, like Bambi, the Disney fawn, and she could ask to borrow a pencil in a way that would leave me speechless. In fact, my inability to hand her a pencil led me to conclude that I was a total failure with girls. Just the sight of a beam of sunlight on the back of her neck as she bent forward over her desk during those drowsy lectures on dangling participles, and my palms would get clammy and my heart would thump, and I could imagine the computers at Mission Control flashing their warning lights while little white-shirted guys in horn-rimmed glasses scrambled around, frantically adjusting knobs and dials.

Now that I've entered college I still react that way to girls. I don't know why. Toeing the edge of the roof that day was, by comparison, a piece of cake. There I was, thirty feet above the ground, playing chicken with gravity and practicing heart-rate control—arms extended, eyes closed, thinking, *calm, calm, calm.* And sure enough, after a while I could feel it—the calm overtaking me, the hypnotic summer sounds of mockingbirds and droning bees and the warmth itself receding to some place in the back of my mind. I stood somewhere outside my body, totally alone. All the world had been reduced to the sound of my own breath, the movement of air, the filling of space. And then, after what seemed like a long while, someone tapped me on the shoulder and said, "Dude."

I didn't expect it. I inhaled quickly and felt myself lunge upward, and my arms flew forward in an arc, and I sensed my body launching into the air. But something held me back—a single arm across my chest. I sprawled backward onto the shingles and opened my eyes, and in the sun's glare I made out a blond-haired, blue-eyed guy beside me. He wore jeans, combat boots, no shirt. His hair was long and curly, his skin deeply tanned. And oddly enough, he looked not at me but at the landscape—at what was left of the old farm where we were building our house. After a while he spit a glob of saliva over the edge of the roof, then glanced at me. "So," he said. "What the hell's wrong with you?"

I shrugged. "Nothing," I said. "I was, like, training. To be an astronaut. You know."

He grunted and looked at the landscape.

"Well. I guess I ought to be right proud to meet you, then," he said, still looking away. His voice was low and very slow. "My name's Webb." He grinned, almost a grimace. "I'm training to be a member of the planet earth." He looked at me, grinned quickly again, then grew somber. There was a long silence. It was almost like he was waiting for me to reach out, to take his hand. Finally he walked a few feet away, scratched his crotch, and began nailing shingles to the roof.

And he nailed steadily all day long. I scrambled along with him, working more efficiently than I ever had before. For some reason I felt I had to prove to this guy that I was at least as good a worker as he was—and at the same time, somewhere deep inside myself, I resented his intrusion into my space. About all I could get out of him the entire day was that Father had hired him to help with the roof. He wouldn't say much else.

■

I operate on the principle that any ordinary individual can become an astronaut. That's the beauty of it—it's democratic. Things like race, sex,

131

or creed are not really important. What matters is what you're made of, because when it comes to being an astronaut, all men are created equal. Everybody has a chance, which is what the Founding Fathers intended. Pride and perseverance—that's what it takes. You have to stick to a job no matter what. And that's one thing that I will always admire about Webb—how he worked until the job was done. For three days we worked on that roof, from dawn to sunset, and on the fourth day, early in the afternoon, the job was finished, right down to the final details of cleaning away the discarded shingles and putting away the tools. And it was only then—only after the job was done and Webb had folded two twenty-dollar bills from Father into his jeans pocket, and Father had said, "Thanks again, take care," and walked away from us, leaving me and Webb standing in the red-mud scrape of gravely earth beside the house, staring at that house like it had sprung up out of the mud on its own and now was about to blast off into space—it was only then that Webb revealed a bit of who he really was. "Come on, man," he said to me, grinning. "Let's party."

"Party?"

"Yeah, party. Come on. Let's have a little fun." He put his hands in his pockets, hunched his shoulders, and jerked his head toward the woods behind us. "Out at my place." And then he looked in my eyes and leaned close, so close I could smell his breath like some kind of dead something, and in a low voice he said, "I got these chicks, man. I got these really good-looking chicks." He grinned and winked one bloodshot eye.

I looked at the woods and then over my shoulder at Father, who went inside the house. "I don't know," I said. "I've things to do."

"Come on, man," he said. "What are you, some kind of pussy?" I didn't reply, so he said, "Yeah, that's it. You're some kind of candy-ass pussy."

It occurred to me that this was the first time Webb had ever spoken to me about anything other than roofing. And of course, at that time in my life I was not accustomed to such raw language. But somehow I knew I'd been challenged. And I was perfectly aware that accepting such a challenge might not be wise. But we learn from our mistakes, so that one day, we will obliterate all possibility of their occurrence—something an astronaut must work toward. Just let me say this; if a billion years ago some ancestral fish hadn't crept from the primordial soup of an ancient sea into the alien terrestrial landscape, if he hadn't taken a chance, the human race would not exist. Without alien worlds to dare into and conquer, we get stagnant, like water behind a dam.

Besides, I was interested in meeting girls. So I fell in behind him as he crossed our yard. I said, "Okay, okay, I'll come along, for a while anyway. Perhaps you can get me a date with one of those girls you mentioned."

He stopped when I said that. We were at the edge of our property, right where the thick undergrowth began. He turned to look at me. "A date?" He grinned and said, "I like you, man. I mean, really." Then he laughed. "A date." He turned, pushing through high weeds, and stepped onto a small footpath hidden behind some honeysuckle. I followed him into the woods.

■

At that point all I knew about Webb was what Father had told me on the very first day. After Webb had gone home, I said, "Where'd he come from Father? Where'd you find him?"

"Who?" said Father. He was counting bundles of shingles, his lips moving silently as he counted.

"That Webb fellow."

Father shrugged. "He's one of the Dentons," he said. "And he's one of the good ones, too. Like his daddy was—Hamp Denton. Good Christian people, salt of the earth."

I nodded. Father knew most everybody out here in this part of the county. It's where he grew up. He pulled a slip of paper from his pocket and wrote something on it, then ran his fingers through his silver hair. "You know, Hamp Denton went to war, and *fought* in it," he said. He looked off into the woods. "No prissing around feeling sorry for himself. Soldiers were soldiers back then. And it's the same with his boys. You could learn a thing or two from Webb, son. About work. About pulling your own weight in this world."

I didn't say anything.

"They're not all like that," said Father. "Many of the Dentons are trash. But Webb, he's one of the good ones."

I hoped so. The whole reason for building a house in the country was to be around "the good ones" of the world. That was the whole idea. Life in the suburbs had finally got to be too much for Father. The riots downtown, the traffic jams, noisy neighbors—he couldn't take it anymore. The final straw was when the government threatened to bus kids from downtown Chattanooga to our schools in East Ridge, bringing inner-city troublemakers to our community and taking kids like me to those bombed-out schools downtown. The very week the busing plan hit the papers, Father bought land in the country—one acre of a huge, abandoned farm at Bucktooth Haven, a few miles north of Chattanooga, near Hixson, Father's hometown.

The land had seemed secluded enough, and quite peaceful. It was alongside a road that had been built for access to the new nuclear power plant, which was under construction about a mile away—a convenient location, really, since Father worked there in public relations.

One morning back in the winter, when we were still framing the walls of our new house, we found that a truckload of insulation had been ripped to shreds. "I hate to use the word," Father told me, "but those niggers did that."

"Really?"

"Yeah. There's a bunch of 'em out here, son. You'll see them in little shanties if you go down the new road here and take a right on Maloney. Now, they're good folks, mostly, don't get me wrong—coloreds here in the country aren't like those downtown. But there's a bad apple everywhere, I guess, and these days some people aren't satisfied with what life hands them."

"Yes sir."

"Don't go down there, son. Stay away from Maloney Road."

"Yes sir, Father."

Father called the County Sheriff's office and convinced a patrolman, who was a relative of ours, to drive by Maloney Road and hand those people a warning, and that was the end of that. Things went smoothly from then on. Time passed, summer came, and soon I forgot all about it.

■

"I made this trail myself," Webb said. "You know how?"

"How?" I asked absently. We were only a few steps into the woods behind the house, just over the property line. I was still wearing my tool-apron, jammed full of roofing nails.

Webb stepped behind a cedar, then jumped quickly back onto the trail and spun toward me. He had a sword in his hands. He held it high above his head and lunged at me, giving a yell that matched the way his eyes looked—suddenly wild, stabbing and hard like shards of ice. I guess I backed up or something, but I don't remember for sure; all I remember is falling backward, flat on my butt, and then trying to raise my feet into the air, as though that would stop him from doing whatever he was about to do. But my feet were tangled in something. I couldn't lift them. Webb swung the sword above me. It made a sound like the wings of a bird hovering above water. I tried again to lift my feet, and I felt something digging tight into my left ankle, sharp and tight. I looked down and saw a strand of barbed wire, scabbed with rust, tangled around me. Nails were scattered across the leaves. Webb stood over me, swinging the sword, fast now, in tight loops like the turns of a maple seed falling to the ground, bringing it so close I could feel air moving on my sweat, cool and soft. Then he stopped, lowered the sword, and laughed.

"Yeah," said Webb. "Pretty good, huh? I made the path myself. With this sword." He laughed again. "And you know, this sword is really old. I wonder how many heads got chopped with it, in its day." He ran his finger long the blade thoughtfully. Suddenly he swung at a dogwood limb, severing it cleanly with one blow. He laughed, then looked at me. "Aw, man, scared the bejesus out of you, didn't I?" He reached down and took my arm, helping me up. "Sorry, Dude. Didn't mean anything by it."

"I wasn't scared," I said. I wiped my forehead with the sleeve of my shirt. "Not really." I bent down and extracted my ankles from the barbed wire. There were small punctures on the shin of my left leg.

"Then come on, Dude," Webb said. He turned and walked along the path again, swinging the sword at foliage.

I hesitated. "I'm not sure coming with you now would be a good idea," I said. "Maybe some other time."

"Not a good idea?"

"Yeah, you know. Not wise. Not smart. Not prudent."

"Oh. Oh, yeah. Prudent." He laughed. "Prudence is dead, man."

He began singing, "Dear Prudence, won't you come out to play?" Then for no apparent reason he seemed suddenly angry, swinging the sword wildly into the tall weeds and saplings. "Come on, man. What's wrong? You chicken? You some kind of pussy?"

I didn't answer, and he kept swinging the sword, harder now. Leaves fell to the ground, green and soft. He stopped and turned to me, holding the sword in front of him, in both hands. He said, "Oh, yeah, I almost forgot. You're an astronaut." He started hacking at the weeds again, walking away now. "You're a precious fuckin' astronaut."

And that's when the girl appeared. That's the only word for it— she simply appeared, as though she had been there all along but only now had suddenly decided to reflect light. She was tall, tanned, muscular looking, wearing small pink shorts and a halter top. She was on the trail between Webb and me, but Webb didn't see her. I watched her chase after Webb and jump on his back. She giggled, her arms draped over his shoulders, her legs around his waist.

Webb dropped the sword and started spinning around. She covered his eyes with her hands. She's still giggling, her teeth flashing, her eyes like light. His face is distorted and red as he spins, bumping into trees and stumbling through weeds, and she's laughing and he's spinning, clearly not laughing, until finally he buckles his knees and leans backward, dropping her onto her back in the weeds. Then he turns over and grabs her wrists, pinning her to the ground, and he's laughing now. And they kiss. A long, sloppy one. Finally he lets her up, both of them red-faced and sweaty, and it's like I'm not even there—she laughs again and jabs him in the belly and takes off down the trail, and he scrambles up, grabs the sword, and takes off after her, out of sight. And for no clear reason, I followed.

■

Then I met another girl. She was standing alone in sunlight, about ten feet from me, where the trail opened into the clearing near the barn. Her arms rested on top of an old fence post; she balanced herself there with one leg stretched high into the air, toes pointed like a ballerina. Her head was held back, her face to the sky, in profile. She seemed chiseled there in the bright sunlight of the clearing, like a delicate swath of sculpted wood. And the biggest surprise was that, except for a small pair of cutoff jeans, she was naked.

"Hi," she said, without looking at me. Then she began moving her leg methodically, down, then up, then down again. "You must be Walter."

She lowered her leg, turned slightly, and began with the other leg. "I'm Iris," she said. Again she tilted her face toward the sky, as though there was something there nobody else could see. After a moment she stopped her exercise and turned to face me. Her eyes were green and very bright, and there were beads of perspiration on her forehead. "Webb said you were coming," she said. She took two steps forward, then bent at the waist and touched her toes, keeping her knees locked. "He says you're stupid," she said. She stood straight again and looked at me, expressionless. "Are you?"

I said nothing. There were freckles on her face, and her hair, pulled back in a ponytail, was a sandy-red, dusty color. Strands of it had pulled free of the ponytail, falling across her forehead. Her cheeks were flushed from exercise. I looked at her breasts.

"Do you dance?" she asked.

"No. That is, yes."

"I dance quite a lot," she said, matter-of-factly. We were silent as she continued her exercise. I stared, but she ignored me. After a while she pulled on a T-shirt and started across the clearing. "Come with me," she said.

I followed a few feet behind her, in total silence. We went around the barn to a well-worn trail—an overgrown wagon road, really, with a worn path in one rut—that led through dense woods. Finally it opened onto a narrow, curving, graveled roadway. I hesitated there, in the edge of the woods; the road was lined with forest in both directions. Iris stood in the road looking back at me, gave a quick smile, and continued on, faster now. "Come along, Walter," she said. "Don't stand gaping like an ape." She didn't look back to see if I was coming; it was as though she knew I would—as though I were some kind of brainless dolt who would do what she said, no matter what. That galled me, it really did. But I followed. Because the fact is, she was the most beautiful individual I'd ever seen in my life.

That's one of my weaknesses, I guess—my tendency to follow beautiful women. If I'm to be an astronaut, that's something I'll have to work on.

■

After about a quarter of a mile the road topped a hill, and there's this old guy in the road, looking into the woods, his hands in his overalls' pockets. He doesn't seem to notice us.

"Hi, Pops," says Iris as she passes him. He says nothing, doesn't move. When I pass, I notice he's glassy-eyed, looking lost, like someone waiting on a bus in an unfamiliar neighborhood. Unlaced boots, no shirt; one leg of his overalls is cut just below the knee, jagged and stringy, as though tailored with an axe; the other pant leg is much too long, dragging the ground. After I pass him, he yells, "Hey!"

I look back. He's still staring into the woods. "Hey!" he says to the trees in a painful, strained voice. "Them cattle! Them cattle's jumping higher than I ever seen cattle jump." He laughs. "Don't run away, now! Don't run away."

I look at Iris. She's walking, still very fast, ignoring me and the old man. So I continue, watching the sway of her hips. The road curves, and I look back one last time. The old man is still standing there, staring into the woods, smiling now.

■

Around the curve is a tar-paper shack. The road ends there, in a big mud clearing without a speck of grass. There's a broken-down tractor, a wrecked Packard with a tree growing through the windshield, a rusty trash barrel with wisps of smoke coming from it. A typical Bucktooth Haven house. Iris just marches right up to the cabin and opens the door, and at this point I'm thinking about Third World training—the way they take astronauts to places like, say, the Polynesian Islands, or maybe Africa or Mexico, so they can teach them how to survive in remote, backward places. After all, one day the astronauts may reenter the atmosphere on Emergency Trajectory, splash down in some remote place, and wash up on the wrong continent. Anything could happen to an astronaut.

Iris stands in a beam of late evening sun in the open door, watching me. Her hair is loose now, her pink face floating in a mass of hair, bright and weightless. I look in her eyes and she turns away, and I follow her into the blackness of the cabin.

The room is windowless and dark and there is a strangely pungent odor in the air. I hear a television, but the sound is garbled. Then I see the TV across the room, flashing a pale blue glow into smoky air. It's John Wayne as an infantryman, leading GIs across a beach, goading them to their deaths with his heavy, furrowed stare.

The door slams behind me. I spin around and there's Webb's face stuck right in mine, his big toothy grin floating disembodied in the darkness like a moon; smoke streams from his nose and from his smile, his skin pale blue from TV glow. "Well," he says. "Well, well, well. It's little Walter."

He moves beside me, puts his arm around my shoulder, and leads me toward the center of the room.

"Tell me, Walter," he says. "Do you like it here?"

"Where? Right here?"

"Bucktooth Haven, dumbass. How do you like Bucktooth Haven? I mean, so far."

"Oh, just fine. It's nice here."

"Well, don't worry, it'll grow on you."

I heard a girl laugh. In the darkness I could make out a sofa beside the television. Webb's girlfriend sat on the sofa, right in the middle of it. Oddly, the television faced the center of the room; anyone sitting on the sofa could not see it.

"He says it's nice here," she said, laughing some more. "Come here, Walter. Come over here. Sit by me." She patted the sofa. "Come."

"Go on, Walter," said Webb. "Sit by Jane. Jane wants you to sit by her."

"Come," she said. "Don't be bashful."

"Go on, Walter."

"Right now, Walter."

I walked to the sofa and sat beside her. She put her arm around my shoulder. "Relax, Walter. Relax." She laughed again. "Webb tells me you're going to be an astronaut." She put a cigarette to her lips, inhaled deeply, then extended it to me. "Here," she said, in a strained voice, holding the cigarette in front of my face. "Try this."

I noticed she was not exhaling the smoke. She was obviously trying to hold it in as long as possible. I looked carefully at the cigarette. "Is that a marijuana cigarette?" I said, watching smoke snake from it, wrapping around her fingers in graceful curls. "No offense, Jane, but I really shouldn't participate in smoking marijuana cigarettes. Really. It wouldn't be wise."

She spewed all the smoke from her lungs at once and began laughing. Webb was laughing too. He was on the floor in front of the sofa, lying on his back, laughing, and it went on for what seemed like forever, until Jane finally got her composure enough to say, "Pretty please, Walter. Just one little puff?"

I said, "No, thank you. Seriously. I can't tell you how important it is that I remain drug-free." And they both went into more hysterics.

I felt deeply embarrassed. I tried to rise from the sofa, but Jane kept her arm around my shoulder, and said, "Please, Walter. Please stay." So I leaned back, and she pulled herself closer to me, and the room grew quiet. The only sound was gunfire, garbled and frantic, from the TV set. It sent strange flashes of light across the room, which, as best as I could tell, was full of cardboard boxes.

"Well!" I said, as cheerfully as I could.

Suddenly Webb stood over me. "Take the joint, Walter," he said. "Take it."

I just looked at him.

"You think I'm joking?" He snickered. "Come on, you coward." He seemed serious now. Jane held the joint in my face again. I noticed her fingernails. They were very long, a pink color, with a different colored star on each one. I looked at Jane's face. It was all but hidden behind her long, blond hair.

Then came the sword, the tip of it. Webb held it against my nose, right between the nostrils. I leaned my head back against the sofa as he pressed the sword firmly against my skin. "Take the joint," he said. I could smell the sword, a deep, cold smell, like a well.

"Take it. Now."

Jane snickered and said, "Forget it, Webb. He's out of it."

"I said take it!" He was yelling now. I reached out, but I didn't know where the joint was. All I could see was the sword, the long, silver trail of it. It pushed harder against my skin, painful now. I flailed blindly into the air. "Take it!"

Then a hand appeared and gently brushed the sword aside. I let out a long sigh and saw Iris's face floating in the murky dimness of the room, a calm face—expressionless, radiant, like a white cloud against a thunderhead. She sat on my lap, and I could feel the pulse of her, the warmth of her as she moved her mouth close to mine, pursing her lips into a red, wet O. She placed the joint there—backward inside her mouth, with the fire side in—leaving a bit of it protruding from her lips. She closed her eyes, moved closer, and blew.

Jane laughed and said, "Suck, Walter, suck!"

Iris's arms were around me, her lips against mine. She ran her fingers in circles across my ear lobes. Smoke filled my nostrils. My mouth flew open and smoke filled it, too. My vital signs grew chaotic.

"Shotgun!" yelled Webb, laughing. "Go for it, Dude."

Iris's hands were in my hair now, running through it gently. The smoke was like some living thing passing between us, and that moment seemed to go on forever. But in just a few seconds I was coughing uncontrollably. Iris raised up, pulled my head to her breast, and held me there, and I coughed for a long, long time, with tears running down my face. I could hear Webb and Jane laughing, and the mangled voice of John Wayne droning on and on, and I could hear Webb saying "Go for it, Walter, go for it." But Webb seemed far away, in some other world.

After a while, the front door opened and the room was flooded with light, and my body went tense. It was an adult—the old man, the one we'd passed on the road—and Iris didn't even move from my lap.

"Hi, Pops," said Iris, brightly. She took a long drag on the joint, and passed it to Webb, who was leaning on the arm of the sofa beside us.

"Granddad," Webb said. "I'd like you to meet Walter, an astronaut. Walter, my grandfather, Hiram Denton, also an astronaut."

The girls began laughing.

"I'm not an astronaut at all, Mr. Denton. But I'm glad to meet you, sir."

They laughed at that, too.

"Isn't he modest?" said Webb. He inhaled from the joint, which was tiny now, then dropped it to the floor. He went over to Mr. Denton, still in the doorway. "Look," Webb said, holding the palm of his hand in front of the old man's face. "Hey diddle, diddle," he said, pointing as though reading from his palm. *"The cat,"* he said slowly. *"And the fiddle."* Mr. Denton's eyes were fixed intently on Webb's palm.

Jane was laughing again. But Iris quietly rose from my lap and crossed the room.

"The cow," said Webb. Then he dropped his hand and put his arm around Mr. Denton's shoulder. *"The cow.* What about the cow, Pops? Tell us about the cow."

"It's gonna rain," said the old man, his voice thin, wheezy. "And there's so much to do."

"Pops," said Iris. She took his hand. "Come with me. Your dinner's ready."

But Webb kept his arm around the old man. "No, wait. Tell us about the cow. Walter wants to hear about the cow."

I shrugged. "If Mr. Denton would rather eat his dinner—"

"Shut up," said Webb. *"The cow,* Pops."

The old man looked at me. "Them cattle," said the old man slowly. "They jump. Up." He looked at the ceiling, one hand rising into the air. "Higher than you'd believe, just soaring into the sky. Up.

Up. And away." His arm moved from side to side, as though wiping the room away.

Jane began laughing uncontrollably on the sofa next to me. She stretched her legs across my lap, covering her eyes with her arm as she laughed, on and on and on. Webb looked at me and pointed his thumb at the old man. "He's a trip," said Webb. He laughed. "Ain't he a trip?"

"Come," said Iris, her face as expressionless as her voice. She led the old man to another room.

"He's my ticket from 'Nam, that's what he is," said Webb.

Jane kept laughing, holding her belly now, but suddenly Webb wasn't laughing at all. He was squatting in the doorway, face in his hands, staring at the floor. After a while I stepped quietly past him, into the sunlight.

"I guess I have to go now," I said.

"Later, Dude." Webb didn't look up.

"Sure," I replied. I looked back into the room. Jane seemed to be sleeping, stretched on the sofa. The TV showed President Nixon now. He stood in front of a map, pointing at it with a baton, talking urgently. Little B-52 bombers were pasted to the map. "My regards to Iris," I said. No one replied. I found my own way home.

■

When I arrived home at sunset, a formal table was set in the dining room, with a white cloth and brass candelabra. This came as a surprise, because the house was not yet finished and we were still spending the nights at our place in the suburbs.

"Walter, please wash and come to table," said Mother. She and Father were already eating Chinese take-out.

"Yes Ma'am," I replied. Washcloths and towels were hanging neatly in the bathroom, which still had a plywood floor.

When I returned they passed food to me in silence. Then Mother said, "Well, Walter. You can explain everything now."

"Now Wanda, leave the boy alone."

She ignored him. "Walter?"

"I've been at Webb's, Mother. We—"

"See, Wanda, he's been with Webb Denton. Now let the boy be."

"Well, I hardly think I'm out of line to ask what they've been doing all this time, am I dear? I mean, really."

"They've been hiking in the woods, haven't you, Walter?"

"Yes sir."

"See? Now let him be." We were silent for a while, listening to the sound of cicadas through the open window.

"Did he show you that Mustang?" Father asked.

"No sir. I saw an old Packard, but no Mustang."

"The Mustang was Mickey's, you know."

"Whose?"

"Mickey's. His brother. He's been dead three years."

"Oh?"

"Vietnam."

"Oh."

"What I like about them Dentons," Father said, forking out more noodles, "is the way they stare tragedy in the face. They've had more than their fair share, but they just stare it down. They're tough. An inspiration, that's what they are."

"Yes sir."

"They stick together. You meet Hiram?"

"Yes sir."

"Haven't seen him in years. I been meaning to get out there and see him." He reached for another eggroll and bit into it.

"You mean Hiram Denton is still alive?" asked Mother. "Heavens! Pass the soy sauce, please."

I passed it to her.

"It seems I remember, from years and years ago, a terrible fire involving the Dentons," she said, conversationally.

"Yeah, and it was right out back here." Father pointed to the back of the house. "Back in those woods somewhere was the old Denton homeplace. A bunch of Dentons died in that fire. Webb's mom included. This land I bought was a part of their back acreage. Our barn was a Denton barn."

"Fascinating," said Mother. "Walter, would you please close the window? There's a draft. You've hardly eaten."

"Yes Ma'am."

"That boy Webb, he's a good boy," said Father. "I went to school with Webb's daddy, Hamp Denton. He died when Webb was a baby. Stepped on a mine in the jungle at Guadalcanal, four years after the war ended."

I pulled the window closed. That's when I noticed the glass was smashed. There was a jagged hole in it, about the size of a pancake.

"Now Webb's taking care of his granddad," Father said, "living with him in one of the old sharecropper cabins. And he's no more than nineteen or twenty."

"Goodness," said Mother. "He must be quite a boy."

"Webb's Uncle Buck looks after them some. He lives in Huntsville, though. You remember Buck, don't you honey?"

"Oh, of course I do," said Mother. "Walter, please eat your dinner."

"Huntsville?" I asked. "You mean, Alabama?"

"Yeah. When Buck retired from the Air Force, he became a businessman. Runs an electronics supply house in Huntsville."

"Does he deal with NASA?" NASA, I knew, had a base in Huntsville, near the old Redstone Missile Arsenal.

Father looked at me thoughtfully. "Yeah, I guess he does. You know, you might do well to get to know these Dentons, son." He stuffed the rest of the eggroll in his mouth. "A boy like you ought to think of the future."

■

I visited Webb and his friends several times in the weeks before school started—sometimes at the cabin, other times in the woods and meadows around it. I went there mainly to observe, the way an astronaut might visit an inhabited planet to observe alien life-forms. I tried not to say much. My social skills, after all, left much to be desired, especially with people like Webb and his friends.

Jane and Iris, it seemed, were always at the Denton place. And I quickly learned that Webb was something of a comedian; his odd behavior and scary actions had a kind of skewed humor, when viewed from the proper angle. But he was a tangle of mystery, too. The fact is, I couldn't get over the idea that he didn't like me—that he hated me, even. He was volatile, confusing; he carried the sword everywhere, hacking new trails across the old farm. Often he was full of anger, as though the very weeds and saplings that choked the farm were choking him, too. Then he'd be as gentle as a lamb, funnier than somebody on the Ed Sullivan show. Maybe it was the marijuana that made him that way. Webb smoked constantly. And you must understand that, although I joined in those marijuana sessions, it was only as an observer: I didn't inhale. To Webb and his friends, smoking was almost a religion; no one was allowed to turn it down—no one, that is, except Iris. She could do as she pleased.

Iris, of course, was the reason I kept going to Webb's. She was distant, though, and even more mysterious than Webb, and I quickly came to realize that she was unattainable—that I could only look. She was always dancing, it seemed, solitary and simple, with an almost weightless grace, floating through woods and fields in wide loops around us while Webb and Jane and I sat together in the sun, the way hippies do, passing the joint among us. There was usually a radio there, too, playing Hendrix, the Stones, that sort of thing. Sometimes Iris would join us in our little circle, sweating, her legs reddened from weed-scrapes, her face covered in a slight, almost inward smile. She'd take a hard drag from the joint and dance away again, her body light like cotton, lofting above the earth like something the planet couldn't convince itself to hold on to.

Sometimes I'd roam the woods behind my house, looking for her, utterly devoid of self-control. One day I stepped from one of Webb's trails into a weedy clearing, and there she was fifty feet from me, dancing naked and alone in high grass beside the ruins of an old chimney. I watched for a while, full of longing and a bit of shame at my cowardice, until at last she grew tired, dressed herself, and disappeared quietly into the woods.

■

Webb told different stories about that sword of his. Once he said his father's grandfather had carried it in the Civil War, when he was one of Nathan Bedford Forrest's cavalrymen, defending honor and the Southern way of life. Another time he said his father had picked it off the dead body of a German officer in a trench outside Berlin in 1945, beside a ruined cathedral.

"Have you ever been in a cathedral?" I said. We were sitting beneath an apple tree in an abandoned grove. I could see Iris about fifty feet away, balancing on her toes with her arms above her head, hands palm to palm.

"What the hell do you think, dumbass?" said Webb. "Of course I've never been in a cathedral. And you haven't either."

"They have vaulted ceilings," I said. "Two-dozen stories high, or more. And you know why?"

"No," said Webb.

"To approximate heaven. Men have always strived for the heavens. The Wright Brothers were just trying to round things off, you know. Trying to fulfill those old dreams."

"Now isn't that peachy?" Webb said. He drew on the joint, smiled, and spread his arms wide. "This is my fucking cathedral, man," he said. "You can keep your vaulted ceilings and your rockets." I looked around. Iris was doing pirouettes beneath the apple trees. After a moment she picked an apple, holding it high in the air. Then she fell to her knees and extended the apple before her in both hands, as though it were King Arthur's chalice. Jane smiled, nuzzling against Webb's chest the way a cat would. I half-expected her to start purring. And it was then that I finally realized what idiots these people were. I knew I had no business hanging around with them, and I vowed to try my best to stay away. I knew it would be tough, though. I couldn't get Iris out of my mind.

■

One day in early September, as we were moving our belongings into the new house, Father said, "You seen Webb, lately, son?"

"Not in several days, sir."

"Did you hear about Iris?"

I dropped the box of books I was carrying: Father knows Iris? "Hear about who?" I said.

"Iris. Webb's twin sister."

My surprise was quickly followed by anger. Why hadn't he mentioned Iris before? Father knew the entire Denton history, but until now he had acted as if she didn't exist.

"Oh, her. Iris. No sir, I didn't hear about Iris." Then I blurted out, without thinking, "And this Jane person. Who is she?"

"Jane? What are you talking about son?" Father set his box down and looked at me. I kept quiet, so he said, "Listen, son. Buck Denton came by yesterday, on business. He says he took Iris to live with him in Huntsville. For her own good. Took Hiram too. That's all I'm saying. I don't know anybody named Jane."

"So Iris lives in Huntsville now?"

He looked worried. "Yeah, that's right, son. With her Uncle Buck." He was talking softly now. "Buck, he's having hard times, you know. And Iris, she needs help too. So Buck put her to work. It'll be good for her, son. You know, straighten her out."

But I wasn't listening. I was still overwhelmed by the news that Iris was Webb's sister. It cast a new light on everything that had happened. After all, Webb had encouraged the development of a relationship between Iris and me, hadn't he? At least he had led me to her. So if he thought I was so stupid, if he didn't like me, what motive could he possibly have had? What had Webb been up to all this time? Father was giving me a funny look, so I picked up the box and went inside.

■

In a way I was relieved that Iris was gone—what my willpower couldn't accomplish, circumstance had accomplished for me. Father said Webb had refused to move to Huntsville; he was still out in that cabin. But with Iris away, there was no reason for me to deal with

151

Webb any longer. Besides, school was again in session, and I was very busy. So I vowed again to forget about Webb, and to forget Iris, too. In the space age, dwelling on the past is the ultimate folly.

So when Father announced that he had finally convinced Webb's Uncle Buck to sell him the rest of the farm, I saw no problem with it. Progress is progress, after all. It's what makes us human. Then, less than three weeks after closing the deal with Buck Denton, Father sold the land to developers from Connecticut at a substantial profit. Soon it was obvious that the developers were planning to build a major subdivision in the overgrown fields behind our house. Surveyors swarmed around for more than two months, taking measurements and putting out a system of fluorescent stakes to mark the boundaries of lots and to show where the roads would go. Men in suits and hard hats marched through the woods carrying large rolls of paper, spreading them out occasionally and talking urgently, pointing in different directions. Then, in late November, the bulldozers came. Mother convinced Father to build a high fence around the backyard—a wooden privacy fence. "We're using redwood lumber in this fence," Father said. "Real redwood, from California. If you're going to do something, son, it's important to do it well. This fence will last forever."

■

I had my last party with Webb on an unseasonably warm afternoon, late in November. I was on the front porch of our house that afternoon, studying for a physics exam, when Webb drove by in his Mustang convertible. He passed the house, then slammed his brakes and backed up, burning rubber in reverse. Jane was in the passenger's seat. She wore dark glasses, and her hair, very long now, was flying in all directions.

"Well, if it isn't Werner Von Braun," he said. "Burn my draft card, Jane, I've decided to become an astronaut."

"Hello, Webb. Jane."

"Get in, Dude."

"Sorry Webb, but I have things to do. Maybe some other time. Besides, your car is a two-seater."

Jane stood, then perched on the back of the seat. "Here, Walter," she said, smiling, "sit between my legs."

"Get in," said Webb. "Just a short ride. There's something I need to show you."

Jane still smiled. When I got in, she wrapped her legs around my shoulders, placing her bare feet in my lap. She wore shorts, her legs bare and stubbly against my cheeks.

"Mind if I call you Werner?" Webb said. Jane giggled.

The car sat still while Webb gunned the engine. "And now, ladies and gentlemen," he said in a fake German accent. "The Commandant Verner Von Braun will cause two-thirds of the people of the planet to disappear before your very eyes, something we in the party have been working toward for many years."

"How?" said Jane.

"By strapping them to a V-2, of course. By shooting all the miserable undesirables into the deepest recesses of space."

Jane ran her hands across the top of my head. I felt hot, sweating between her thighs.

"Or better yet," he said, "Werner will strap himself to the rocket. He'll colonize new worlds. He'll stick his holy head in stellar sand."

Webb gunned the engine and the car jerked forward. The tires squealed; Jane tightened her grip as the car accelerated.

Webb's laughing now. "How about them G-forces, Walter?" he yells. "Like that? 100! 110! Fast enough for you, Walter?"

I close my eyes. Jane is leaning forward, her hair streaming over me, her arms locked around my neck; I feel the pavement end and I open my eyes. The hourglass of the nuclear plant's cooling tower flies toward us; parked trucks, piles of pipes, stacks of lumber fly by as we move in circles around the tower, around and around through a cloud of our own dust, white and acrid, the car bucking and sliding as though the earth itself is pushing against us, Jane clamping her thighs and arms tightly around me, holding hard to me, trembling, screaming something I can't make out, the radio playing "Sergeant Pepper's Lonely Hearts' Club Band" so loud I can't understand what Webb is saying to me. He's yelling, his face contorted in what appears to be uncontrolled rage as the car spins, sliding sideways, the car pulling tighter and closer around the concrete and steel of the cooling tower until we're on the pavement again, gliding, and I sink limp into the seat as the car jerks hard and quick onto one of the new subdivision roads, jolting and jumping through the desolate scrape like the bucking of a mad animal, Jane's screams desperate now, screaming at Webb in anger and fear until at last the car falls to rest.

Surveyor's stakes are piled beside a gray tangle of blackberry and pokeweed. Webb gets out of the car. "I gathered them for you, Walter," Webb says. "All for you." He takes a can of gasoline from the car's trunk and douses the stakes. Jane and I stand watching as he throws a match to it and it flames up. "Breaking a few windows, trashing some insulation, that's just kid's stuff," says Webb. "I have so much more to contribute."

I stared at the flames and remembered my father warning me about the black folks on Maloney Road.

"So you did that, Webb?" I said. "It was you?"

"Yeah," he said. He was calm now, smiling, beatific. "I did the insulation thing. Like it? I used the sword, of course. I didn't vandalize, Walter. I carved."

"But why? Why did you do it?"

"For the same reason I'm burning these stakes, you asshole." He grabbed my arm and looked straight into my eyes. I could feel him trembling. I glanced at Jane, but she quickly looked away. She was as distant as the trees around us.

"I mean, hell, what do you expect, man?" Webb's voice rose like a hard wind. For a moment I thought I saw fear in his eyes.

I looked at the burning pile of stakes. Flames were inching into the weeds.

"Father thought the Negroes did it," I said. "I mean, he thought Negroes vandalized the house."

Webb let go of my arm. He seemed to relax. "Yeah, well, the niggers did do it."

"But you said—"

"I did it, the niggers did it. Whatever. It's all the same thing. You see, a man like your father needs his niggers, so I'm his niggers. I see it as my civic duty." Jane put her arms around him from behind. "Somebody's got to do it, Walter."

Then I realized his problem. He couldn't see the big picture. I thought of photographs of our globe, blue and alone in the darkness of the universe—the scale of the whole thing. "Look," I said. "What does it matter in the long run? You need a new perspective on things, a new angle. What does this little patch of ground really amount to?"

"Space," he said, absently, eyes on the ground. Jane hugged him from behind, rubbing her hands across his chest. "Let's go, Webb," she said. "Come on."

I shrugged. "The world's a big place, Webb."

Then he suddenly began coughing, a kind of angry, spitting cough, and it took a moment for me to realize that he was actually trying to speak.

"Let's go, Webb," said Jane. "Forget it."

He pushed her away, but she came back to him. "You think—" he said, "you actually think—"

He looked away and laughed one sharp laugh, hard like an ice pick through ice, as though everything I'd been saying—indeed, everything I *am*—was so absurd it was impossible for him to reply any further. He shook his head and smiled an angry kind of grimace-smile, shaking his head over and over, saying "Man, man" in a tone of disbelief, shifting his weight from foot to foot, his eyes everywhere but on me.

So I turned from him. I walked along the bulldozed scar through the woods, toward two trucks sitting about a hundred feet away. I knew a trail must cross near there, a trail that would lead home. And as I was passing the trucks, I noticed their tires were slashed. I saw Webb's sword there, lying in the dirt.

"Pick it up, Walter." Webb had followed me. He pushed me in the small of the back. "Pick it up!" I turned. He was smiling, a nauseating smile. Smoke filled the air behind him. He stepped forward and pushed me again. "There's a good tire left on that GMC," he said. "Pick up the sword, Walter. Slash it. What's wrong? You a pussy?"

I could smell smoke. Webb shoved me again, and I stepped backward. He kept coming at me. "Go on, Verner, take the sword. It's just a tire. What good is it? This is the space age!" His eyes were like pits, his sneering lips spread back across yellowed teeth. I was sick of him now. When I took the sword he laughed and slapped me on the back. "Go on, do it," he said. "What's wrong? Think you'll get in trouble, Walter? Hell, you're a fuckin' astronaut! If there's trouble you can just blast off!"

I stared at the tire, the mud on it, the gravel stuck in the heavy tread. My eyes were stinging from smoke. I felt anger well up in me, anger at Webb and everything connected with the idea of Webb; anger at the way disrespect and chaos seemed to be what he lived for, revelled in, made a faith of. And he kept pushing me.

Clearly I was not in possession of my senses, because what I did then seemed, at the time, inevitable, perfectly normal, even necessary: I yelled at Webb—I don't remember what I yelled, but I yelled—and I jabbed the sword into the tire. It barely made a prick, so I yanked back and jabbed again, throwing my weight into it, feeling it sink into the rubber as I strained to push it deeper. Finally there was a hissing sound as the tire deflated. And instantly I felt like a fool. I heard Jane's nervous laughter as Webb fell to his knees in the dirt and bowed to me, over and over. He, too, began laughing. I tried to pull the sword from the tire, but it wouldn't budge. Jane and Webb walked away, arm in arm, as I pulled uselessly on the sword. Finally I ran along the trail toward home.

When I came to the redwood fence at our yard, thick smoke was blowing in the trees. I went through the gate and into the house, and from my bedroom window I watched silent flames move across the overgrown fields of the old farm. Oddly, the fire never touched the barn, even though it burned in the weeds and trees around it for almost twenty-four hours. Our house was saved by volunteer firefighters from Bucktooth Haven.

■

Father got me off the hook entirely. He fixed things with the county police, one of whom was a relative of ours. I didn't even know I was a suspect until a deal had been made. It happened on Christmas Eve, three weeks after the fire.

It was the same Christmas that *Apollo 8* circled the moon. I was in the living room in front of the TV, waiting for the live coverage of the spaceflight to begin, but I had turned the volume down low because Mother and Father were arguing in the kitchen. I could hear the rise and fall of their voices, but I couldn't make out the words.

Bits of tinsel fell from our Christmas tree. A squirrel was hiding in it, scared to come out. He had fallen down the chimney earlier that day. I walked to the front door and turned on the outside light. Raindrops were falling in the darkness, and the ones falling close by, near the light, were shiny white, like little streaks of ice. I crossed the room to the Christmas tree and knelt in front of it, thinking I would try to shoo the squirrel across the room to the open door. I parted the branches of the tree and peered inside. There he sat with his beady eyes and his pulsing throat, perched on a branch at eye level about three feet away. I'd never seen a squirrel so calm before. Usually a squirrel is a bundle of nerves, but this one just sat there, as if being trapped in our alien world brought out the best in him. I had to shake the tree three times before he would budge, and finally he scooted to the end of a branch, jumped to the wall, and scurried up it, freezing dead still in the cobwebs near the molding. I hit the wall with the palms of my hands. The squirrel shifted quickly but held his ground, clinging to the wall mysteriously. Then, as I was about to give up, the squirrel leaped for the open door and floated across the room as if he were weightless, with his legs outstretched like little wings. He floated out into the night, slowly, beautifully, gliding with unbelievable grace into the darkness.

■

Father was easy with me, really. He came in while the astronauts were taking turns reading from the book of Genesis. The TV showed

158

the earth rising above the lunar surface. It was the first earthrise ever. "And the earth was without form, and void," said an astronaut. "And darkness was upon the face of the deep." There was so much static I could barely make it out.

"You're damn lucky your Uncle Manny's with the county police," said Father. "You listening to me, boy?"

"Yes sir."

"That Denton boy turns out to be trash after all," Father said. "Trash is trash, and Webb is a big pile of trash, and all the worse for acting like he wasn't. I prefer a Denton that acts shiftless and lazy to one that acts like he's really on the ball, only to turn around and fool you. There ain't nothing worse than that."

"Yes sir."

The TV was showing the astronauts huddled together, their faces unshaven. The Bible was passed, weightless, from one astronaut to another. We were quiet for a while, with just the astronauts talking. "And God called the dry land Earth," said the astronaut. "And the gathering together of the waters called he Seas: and God saw that it was good." He closed the Bible. A toothbrush floated by.

"Roger," said Mission Control. "We copy."

■

Just after Christmas I was offered a nice scholarship to the engineering program at M.I.T.—a decent start on my way to the launchpad. The last time I saw Webb was about a week later, on a science club trip to the county prison. Some wiseacre had decided it would be a neat gag to dress in prison garb and get our yearbook picture taken behind razor wire, making little rocks out of big ones. Just before we left, a guard gave us a tour of a cellblock that was supposed to be empty, but there was somebody asleep in a cell at the end of the hallway, his back to us. As the club members were filing by, the inmate turned over and sat up.

"Dude!" he said.

"Webb?"

"What's up, Dude?"

I held to the bars, looking at him. The rest of the boys filed past. Finally he said, "Hey, don't sweat it, man." He shrugged and smiled. "It sure beats the hell out of Vietnam." Then he lay back down and turned to the wall, and I never saw him again.

■

I guess Webb's the kind of guy they mean when they say some people can't cope with this modern world of ours. Of course, being a prospective astronaut, I'm not like Webb at all, because astronauts are the elite of the elite. People look to astronauts for answers—people a lot like Webb and Jane and Iris, poor souls who have lost their way.

Astronauts have a special responsibility to the downtrodden of the earth. That's as much a part of being an astronaut as weightlessness or cosmic radiation. But the thing is, what will I say to people when they come to me for answers? What can I say that will help?

Well, I guess I'll just have to keep my head on straight, keep my perspective. I'll say that one day we'll colonize the moon as a base for exploring other worlds. After all, our long-term mission as astronauts is to find new worlds for the human race to live in, because things here on earth just can't be fixed. Iris, Jane, Webb—if people like that are not part of the team, I'll say, then at least they should be proud to have known someone who is. It's no small thing to have known one of the men who can pave the way for people to follow, who can offer mankind hope.

I'll tell them that each day of our lives is another day of training for the hard travels ahead. Every tough situation, every bump on the road, every hardship we encounter—it's all there for a reason; and if we work hard to keep a no-nonsense, can-do attitude, things will only be easier for us when life seems impossible somewhere down the road. I'll say that no matter what we choose to do with our time on this planet, we are trapped in a continuous process of development; we are all getting ready for something, something really big, whether we know it or not. In fact, it occurs to me now that, in a way, we are all training to be astronauts, constantly, day in and day out, in spite of ourselves. Yeah, that's the kind of thing I'll tell them. They'll like that. It will put their minds at ease.

The Author

Photo by Diane Fox

Brian Griffin grew up in the country near Soddy-Daisy, Tennessee, in a family he describes as "infested by preachers, all Southern Baptists of the fundamentalist sort." He earned his B.A. in English from Middle Tennessee State University and his M.F.A. from the University of Virginia in Charlottesville. Griffin teaches creative writing at the University of Tennessee. He lives with his wife and children in Knoxville and works closely with a group there to promote interracial harmony in the inner city. Griffin's stories and poems have been well published in journals including *Shenandoah*, *New Delta Review*, *Clockwatch Review*, *Snake Nation Review*, and *Southern Poetry Review*. In addition to various short stories and poems, Griffin is currently at work on a novel.